FOREVER AND ALWAYS

MOLLIE MATHEWS

Blue Orchid
PUBLISHING

ABOUT THIS BOOK

Will both Lily and Leonardo end up giving their hearts to the wrong person?

Still reeling following her malicious sacking, family therapist Lily Rose is feeling rejected and low in spirits. Even worse, she's broke. The last thing she needs is more money woes. Which is exactly what happens when she collides with billionaire water magnate Leonardo Ermenegildo Bressolini's mint-condition Lamborghini.

Having found at last a place to retreat from the madness and greed and malevolence of his ex-wife the last thing Leonardo wants is complications. But he is a man in need of a housekeeper. And Lily Rose owes him. Big time.

What both don't know is just what a massive impact the crash will have on their lives. Sparks heat into a collision of powerful forces that cannot be restrained.

Love on the beach sends deep passions and emotional connection—more heartfelt than either has ever known—steaming to the surface.

When Leonardo's past comes careering into his future—

will both Lily and Leonardo end up giving their hearts to the wrong person?

Forever and Always is a short story, clean romance, full of quirky humor and the promise of a happily ever after.

Set in The Bay of Islands, New Zealand—my home—one of the most beautiful, unspoiled paradises in the world.

PRAISE FOR FOREVER AND ALWAYS

"Did you ever dream that a car crash that wiped out your bank account could turn into one of the best days of your life? Meet Lily Rose, who only wants to help children through emotional trauma and ends up finding herself and her true love in the process. This charming and warm short story is just the start of great things to come."

~ Elaine Zieroth

"While a quick read, there's plenty of meat to *Forever and Always* and a happily ever after in the offering!"

~ JoAnn Weiss

"I enjoyed *Forever and Always*—a story about two wounded people that come together in a crash. I very much enjoy Mollie Mathews writing. When she writes I feel like I'm right there because of the colorful descriptions that she paints. I couldn't put it down."

~ Pat

"You will love Lily and Leonardo in this heartwarming short and sweet, modern day tale of seduction. I did."

~ Leanne Lovegrove

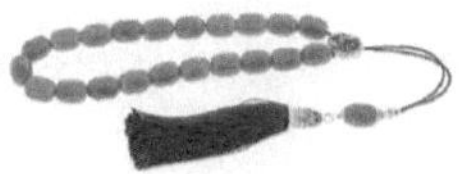

"We all go through hard times in life. It's a part of being alive and it's the reality we all have to deal with. There are times we forget our value as a person because we are so blinded with these thoughts of loneliness, emptiness and ego. Somewhere along the road we become numbed with all the frustrations and dissatisfaction. But life itself isn't always about darkness and sadness, life is also filled with colors and that makes it beautiful. Along this path of darkness there's always light waiting to be seen by our daunted hearts. Our heart is gifted to see this light. It may be hiding behind those circumstances that we encounter; or in a stranger we just met at an unexpected place."

~ Chanda Kaushik

1

"We don't need you anymore." Lavina Embers, Lily Rose's manager of two months, slid a typewritten letter across Lily's desk. "We're letting you go." Her eyes looked through Lily in a cold, detached stare.

Lily stood behind her desk blinking, her heart went eerily still. She looked down at the piece of paper. Her arms felt like they were being peppered by three million sharp nails, as she read the typewritten words.

Friendship House is hereby giving 14 days notice to end your Counselors Contract Agreement.

Her heart took an uncomfortable dive as her mind raced

ahead, trying to comprehend what was happening. "I don't understand." Her stomach heaved like the ocean.

She was being fired. Obviously. But why?

"I thought you were happy with my services."

"There's nothing wrong with your work."

Lavina's tone was warm, almost kind. But her face was stony and unmoving.

Lily inhaled a long, deep breath through her nostrils, then exhaled slowly as she mentally counted to ten. Her chaotic childhood had taught her that it was far better to remain calm in the face of hostility, no matter how insidious the assassin, than to ignite anger.

Breathe. Just breathe.

"What have I done wrong?" Lily said, gently. Of course, her first impulse was to blame herself. Hadn't she learned growing up she was always at fault?

"We don't have to give a reason," Lavina said, coldly.

"What do you mean *you don't have to give a reason?* I thought I was doing good work." Nothing made any sense, even Lily's words came out in a tangle, as she collapsed in her swivel chair. "Has there been a complaint?"

"No. Your clients *love* you."

Was that a slither of envy Lily detected in Lavina's otherwise controlled and measured tone?

"Then why don't you want me anymore?" Lily forced her voice to sound cool, relaxed and measured, but her face burned. "I like it here."

"As I said, we don't have to give a reason."

A wave of righteous anger spiked through Lily's body, jolting her sense of injustice from its shocked slumber. "What do you mean you don't have to give a reason?" She fought to keep her tone from revealing the depth of her anger at the implied assault to her character.

Lavina's tone hardened. "It's in your contract."

Lily clasped her hands in her lap and rubbed her thumb back and forth over the large square citrine ring on her finger. But even the crystal's power couldn't protect her from the negative energy of Lavina's abuse.

Still reeling from the shock of her termination she tried to recall what was written in her contract. Lily didn't do detail, she was a big-picture, blue-skies girl, but even if she had read the fine print nothing could have prepared her for Lavina's unprovoked assault.

Lily glanced down at the letter again, not wanting to believe what now was so obvious.

She wasn't wanted.

She scanned the type-written words looking for a sign that it was a joke, a prank, a silly, funny hoax that they would all laugh about later. But there was no humor hiding in the words running across her eyes in a jumbled blur. She fingered the edges of the termination letter, then slid it away.

She didn't deserve this treatment. She was a good person. She was kind and caring and compassionate.

Bad things didn't happen to good people, she silently affirmed.

Except they did.

They happened all the time. As a counselor, Lily knew this. She knew this only too well.

Surviving her own childhood trauma had drawn her to the profession. She took pride in helping people transcend their pain. She found purpose in listening to their fears. She felt a surge of passion when reminding them that they were much stronger than the poisonous people and events that infected their lives.

And she empathized deeply, their stories were her story.

Their experiences, her experiences too. She loved helping them move from victim to hero in their own lives.

But now this? Why was this happening to her?

There was no warning. Nothing to alert her. No chance to protect herself. Lily glanced over at the poster on the office wall beside her desk. It was a cartoon of a child, but where the child's face should be there was a mirror. Along the bottom of the poster were the words, *'Whose behavior do your kids model?'*

She glanced up at Lavina and then back to the poster. It brought back a long-buried memory of a traumatic incident from her childhood. She had said or done something—what she couldn't remember, all she knew was it had made her father furious.

Perhaps it was her narcissistic mother who had set her father against them like a rabid dog. She was always threatening, "You wait until your father gets home." And then she would be smacked so hard with a wooden spoon it broke.

All she knew right now, at this moment, was that she continued to be at fault.

2

L *ily was always blamed.*
She saw her five-year-old self clutching her younger brother by the hand and fleeing from their home, from the tyranny and rage of their father, from the reach of his wooden spoons. The ones that often splintered and broke with the fury of his attack as the wood met the tender skin of their backsides, legs, or cracked against their skulls.

The sound of Lavina's voice brought her back to the room. "Would you like to leave the building first or would you prefer I do?"

For a brief moment, Lily stared at Lavina, her attention caught by a sheath of cold, indifference.

The wounds now were not physical but emotional. The welts not upon her skin but impregnated in her mind—and Lavina was bringing them all to the surface.

But she'd been so friendly.

Of course, Lily realized with growing disquiet. It had been Lavina's deliberate tactic. Lily should have seen it coming. Narcissists always befriend their empathetic target.

Lily kept her voice cool, as a rush of adrenaline pounded through her, fueled by the injustice and cruelty of her dismissal. "Why would I need you to go first?"

Clearly Lavina was expecting Lily to leave with her tail between her legs and slope away in shame.

Do not let them do this to you, reclaim your power.

Lily set aside her preference to ignore conflict, she shoved away her default program to people-please, she thrust off her deep-rooted belief that she was always at fault, and she pushed back from her desk and rose to her feet.

Lily paused, thrusting her slim shoulders back, she braced herself against the conflict. This wasn't the time to be meek, it wasn't the time to be pathetic.

"My contract may say you don't need to give me an answer, but that's the decent thing to do. We're counselors. We're meant to show caring and compassion."

Her reasonable request was matched with hard, stoic, indifferent silence.

It was as if Lily didn't exist.

Again.

Children should be seen not heard, her father had always said. He'd even wanted her brother and Lily to go and live in the attic.

It didn't matter that she wasn't part of the in-crowd, she told herself firmly. She'd never belonged. Never been accepted. Never been wanted. The fact was she was born that way.

Lily picked up the piece of paper terminating her employment. "Fine. It's your choice. If you say my contract states you need give no reason, I will respect your decision, but you'll have to look into your own soul."

If you have one, she thought.

"You will have to live with how you treated me. You'll have to know that this is a shameful way to treat another human being."

Lavina's lips curved into a savage smirk. "How would you like to hand over your clients?"

My clients. What was she going to say to Sarah, who had been sexually assaulted when she was five? Now 10-years-old the young girl had been referred by her family after threatening to kill herself.

Sarah was only beginning to heal. She had responded well to Lily's empowering creative approach and emphasis on finding ways not to be victimized by other people's cruel and inhumane behavior. The thought of breaking the news to her made Lily's gut clench.

What was she going to say to Max? The 12-year-old boy had been referred for anger management. He had begun his sessions with Lily telling her he felt unloved and unwanted by his mom who had left him behind when she met a new partner. Would Max think Lily was abandoning him too?

Her heart choked.

She rubbed the giant square citrine stone in her ring and pondered how best to respond. An inner voice warned her to tread carefully with this dangerous, unpredictable woman.

"What do *you* want me to say to my clients?" Lily asked.

"We'll say that you decided to move on to greener pastures," Lavina said, in a serrated tone.

Lily wanted to say, "*But that's a lie.*" Instead, she nodded, numbly as she rehearsed trying to deceive her clients in her mind.

Why am I leaving? Oh, I've gone to greener pastures.

It was so cliched. Besides, Lily never was a good liar. She knew her clients would feel let down and betrayed and abandoned.

Lily wanted to tell her clients the truth.

I was fired by an insane witch. But she had absorbed the threat contained in her termination letter. Any breaches of confidentiality, any discussion related to the staff or contractors of Friendship House, would result in legal action.

Her mind spring-boarded to her own fears. It was two weeks before Christmas. There were no greener pastures. How was she going to pay her bills?

Anxiety entangled with guilt. She was putting her own needs first. She should be thinking of her clients. She felt sick.

This isn't happening.

Focus on your breathing, she silently affirmed.

She inhaled a long, deep breath through her nostrils as though she was breathing through a straw—just like she taught her clients.

Get out. Get out. They don't deserve you, a voice urged.

Not before I have my say, she affirmed silently. I'll be damned if I leave conquered, defeated and shamed. I won't give them that victory. I won't let them see how they've hurt me.

I never have. And I never will.

"I will, of course, work out my notice period." Her voice was strong, powerful—betraying nothing of the turmoil she felt inside.

As much as she'd love to tell them to go and shove their

contract, Lily wouldn't let down her existing clients. No way. Whether it was the Master's Degree she held in people pleasing, or some other learned behavior she'd deployed to survive her chaotic childhood she didn't know. All she knew, registering the pained look on Lavina's face, was that Lavina hadn't expected Lily to react so calmly—and it felt good to defy her expectation.

As Lily shut down her computer and gathered her belongings she tried not to think about how she was going to pay her tumultuous credit cards bills—let alone her rent.

"See you tomorrow," she said, faking happiness.

Lily's legs shook as she walked down the stairs leading away from the counseling rooms to the carpark. Her vision blurred as she glanced at the personalized vehicle registration plate which read 'Pas10n' and slid over the writing on the scratched and dented spare wheel hub, 'I'm following my passion—are you?' it read.

Not anymore.

Her fingers trembled as she opened the door to her Honda CRV. Taking care not to hook her dress on the torn leather seats, she climbed behind the wheel and stared blankly ahead as the realization dawned.

All the things that mattered to her—gone. All shattered. In just over 30 seconds.

She wasn't wanted.

Again.

She reached toward her review mirror and unhooked her crystal prayer beads. When would anything go right? she thought as she fingered the violet tassel hanging from the beads.

What she really wished for now more than ever was to work for herself. No more relying on others who could dispose of her so mercilessly. She needed total and absolute control.

As she glanced up at the cloudless sky her thoughts drifted to her stalled idea to start an online business shipping crystal healing remedies all around the world.

It was an impossible dream. As impossible as meeting someone she could trust, someone who wouldn't take her freedom, someone who wanted and loved her unconditionally —forever and always.

She had always been so tirelessly optimistic. Was it time to abandon hope?

3

Leonardo Ermenegildo Bressolini had a new passion and it was making him millions of Euros. Millions and millions and millions, Leonardo thought with satisfaction, as he slid his six-foot-two-inch frame into his pewter gray Lamborghini.

So far his new venture was proving far more lucrative and a damned sight easier than excavating diamonds from the sweltering bowels of one of the many Bressolini diamond mines in Rhodesia.

Water.

Pristine, artesian, water. Liquid diamonds. And found right here in New Zealand, the back seat of the world he'd moved to in search of a place to retreat from the madness and greed and malevolence of people.

Or more specifically, his ex-wife's diamond-digging treachery. The valves in his heart constricted at the memory. It wasn't just his pride that had been destroyed it was his trust in wives. Fatally. Finally. Forever.

Leonardo turned on the ignition and felt his fingers tremble with pleasure as the V12 engine purred like a lioness on heat.

He pulled out and steered his pride and bliss down the long driveway, away from The New Zealand Water Company's head office. Then pushing his calfskin shoe to the floor, accelerated hard. Winding the rooftop down he relished in the exhilaration as his Lamborghini flew down the remote northern road.

His only regret, besides marrying his Ukrainian wife, was not having started his new business line sooner. Diamonds may be a woman's best friend, but water is a necessity, he thought to himself, smiling with satisfaction. And people were consuming his water by the gallons, globally.

It was an absolute winner. One he should've thought of before. But then he hadn't discovered the pristine waters of New Zealand then, had he?

As heir to Italy's premium sparkling water empire, it was where his family had first made its fortune, but now he was claiming an even bigger slice of this wealth. Water was in his veins, but more importantly, as with his other successful ventures, he was pioneering this innovative path on his own.

And on his own he intended to stay. He preferred his personal life that way. Forever and always.

"Lock that marketing blurb in, Ernesto," he said turning to his vice-president who had been patiently waiting in the passenger seat for his boss to leave his office.

"Better water, for a better cause?" Ernesto asked, clarifying his boss's command. He knew better than to speak until he was spoken to, act until he was directed, or offer an opinion without being asked. In all aspects of his business, Leonardo Bressolini was boss—loved as much as he was feared.

"Customers love altruism. They like to know what they're throwing down their necks is making a difference to peoples lives. And it is." Leonardo said with satisfaction as he thought of how many donations he had made to worthy causes and how much employment he had brought to the local community.

Leonardo's grip tightened around the wheel as he thought of his selfish and greedy competitors. Billions of liters of water were siphoned from New Zealand every year for sale overseas, and some of the biggest players, predominantly overseas-based Chinese and Russian companies, paid no fees to use the resource and gave zero back to the communities they pillaged.

Giving back a percentage of profits was not just the right thing to do, it was the only thing to do, he thought. Hadn't he vowed not to be as greedy and selfish as his father who hoarded his wealth and gave nothing away?

"Is it okay, just like it is?" Ernesto asked.

"Read it to me, again," Leonardo commanded in an authoritative Italian accent.

"Water for everyone—giving back to New Zealand communities. A portion of all sales revenue is donated to credible charities which undertake positive initiatives in local communities," Ernesto said.

"Perfecto," Leonardo said, as he sped down the motorway at breakneck speed. The towering voice of Pavarotti singing Frank Sinatra's My Way soared through the air as he gunned the engine of his pride and joy and felt the rush of speed explode through his chest. Powering into the turn off the drive from his manufacturing plant, his tires spat the hot, sticky gravel.

"That'll make the old man squirm in his grave," Leonardo said, relishing in the memories of how his uber conservative and risk adverse father abhorred speed.

"Que?" Ernesto gasped, white knuckling the armrest.

"He never wanted to adopt me, but his neglect did me a favor. He fueled my determination to succeed," Leonardo said, recalling the words of the counselor his wife had forced him to see before they ended their sham of a marriage.

The counselor was as beautiful as she was perceptive. Leonardo's groin stirred at the memory of their first encounter.

Bewitching. Mesmerizing. Dangerous. Seductress. Of course she hadn't meant to be. Some women were just born that way.

He planted his foot down harder and tried to convince himself it was the force of the Lamborghini flying down the road that caused his body to tremble with desire and need.

"My adoptive father gave me everything, the most beautiful Swedish nannies, the finest British education, endless holidays, palatial houses, the legacy of his fortune, and the Colgate smile and the Adonis body to match—the only thing he neglected was to love me," he reached up and gripped the rearview mirror, adjusting it with a firm swipe as he tried to force the hurt that zoomed through his mind like Grand Prix cars approaching from behind.

"His neglect, only fueled my obsession to surround myself with things I love, art, architecture, cars—and my determination to surpass him in my quest for success.

Whoever says money can't buy happiness needs their head read."

"It was love," Ernesto said, placing his hand over his mouth, as he realized his impudence.

"What," Leonardo said, his brows arching in displeasure.

"It was the Beatles," Ernesto stammered.

"Go on."

"Money can't buy you love."

"*Va bene, è la sacrosanta verità.*" It was the gospel truth but it was also a lie. His ex had reminded him all too well of that deception. Money buys you love but, like a fake designer watch or a knockoff of any kind, what it brought more often than not wasn't the real deal, Leonardo mused as he gripped the edge of the steering wheel.

He knew that painfully well. Irritation coursed through his body. His wife loved his money more than him and then tried to load up with other men. Her deceit had blindsided him and he'd been stupid enough to think a trip to a counselor would save their marriage. It was always destined to fail.

As he entered the township of Kerikeri, the largest town in Northland, but mega tiny by European standards, he took his foot off the accelerator and slowed the beast to a purr.

He made his approach to the roundabout and gave way to the approaching cars who had right of way. Speed was fine on the open road, but safety was paramount when it came to lives, especially in towns like this one where anyone at any time could shoot out in front of you.

Leonardo glanced in the rearview mirror, lingering for a moment at his reflection. He'd been told often he was a good looking man, but no one, other than the counselor, had told him the truth.

He did a good job faking happiness.

She had come highly recommended. She was young and

pretty, had long, dark-blond hair, huge green eyes, and her name was Lily. He remembered that she was wearing a long, flowered dress, and a warm smile, as she shook his hand, and introduced herself to his wife—now known as The Old One.

Leonardo had felt immediately drawn to the counselor. And something about her told him that, despite his cynicism, she could make a difference.

He liked what she had to give, the spirit, the hope, the life she radiated. He wanted to believe her. But even she couldn't work miracles.

The Old One, and his marriage was a lost cause.

The experience had hardened him once again to do-gooders, and all things healing. Especially when she turned her scalpel-sharp insights in his direction and tried to slice into his childhood trauma.

He didn't like people getting under his hood, fiddling around with the core of his engine, tampering with his finely tuned mechanics.

The only things that brought Leonardo any comfort was his exotic cars and accelerated earnings—things he could control and which wouldn't give him grief. Anything else left him cold. Which suited him just fine. Money could buy freedom and choices, and right now he chose to be free— now, forever and *always*. *Perfecto.*

"I thought Italians were crazy drivers," Leonardo said, stirring from his thoughts and glancing in his rear mirror again. "But the locals here, they drive cars that are only fit for scrap metal, and they follow too closely." His body bristled with irritation. "Can you see that car, behind us, Ernesto? Any closer and that damned woman will be climbing in my trunk."

4

———

How would it feel to be a billionaire,? Lily wondered as she stared at the back of a pristine, pewter gray Lamborghini which dazzled like diamonds under the late summer sun.

What would it be like to never worry? What would it be like to have everything or anybody you wanted? What would it be like to not wake in the middle of the night in a cold sweat wondering how you were going to pay your rent?

Inconceivable. That's what it would be like.

Lily clenched her worry beads and prayed that something

miraculous would happen and she'd wake up rich. Mega-rich. Mind-blowingly rich.

In your dreams, girl, she thought, but then right now that's all she had—hope on a wing of a prayer.

Lost in her dreams, Lily was drawn in like a magnet by the almost hypnotic allure of the luxury car in front of her as at last the traffic jam freed up and it was their right of way.

Like a beacon of light, its timeless elegance and beauty and strength were an antidote to the mayhem she had just left back in the counseling rooms.

Just looking at the sleek contours of the car gave her soul an immediate uplift. Which didn't surprise her knowing what she did about the power of beauty to help people transcend pain.

Completely oblivious to her following distance she traveled after the dream car as though in a meditative trance.

* * *

"LEONARDO, THE DOG!" Ernesto yelled, gripping the side of his seat and throwing his legs out as though bracing for impact.

With the speed and skill of a Formula One driver Leonardo dropped several gears and braked hard. Both men sighed with relief, and waved to the little boy who ran from the side of the road, and carried the wire-haired fox terrier to safety.

But the relief had barely washed over them when a tremendous jolt shook them both.

"That damn woman has driven into the back of my car."

* * *

This is going to cost a fortune, Lily thought as she studied the smashed taillight, then glanced at the creased and crumpled trunk. Oh, My God. I've just lost my job and now I'm going to lose everything.

Lily's heart raced with the brute horsepower of stampeding stallions. *You'll be fine. You'll be fine,* she said, trying to adopt the same strategies she suggested to her clients when they freaked out. But she wasn't fine. She just wanted to scream.

Sweat dripped down Lily's back and pooled at the base of her spine. The stagnant air in the car grew heavier as she stared straight ahead too stunned to move.

Only drug dealers or pimps can afford cars like the one she'd just hit, she told herself. Would the driver have a gun, would he smash his fist through the window or some other impulsive road rage aggressive and angry behavior? One thing was certain, he would want retribution.

She couldn't breathe. Her heart was pounding so loud she could hear it thrashing against the cavity of her chest. Lily was sure she was going to black out.

I'm having a heart attack. I am dying. At least I won't be worthless anymore, she thought to herself.

Get a grip. Fast.

She breathed in deeply for a count of four and exhaled— slowing for a count of eight. And began to repeat 10 times for optimal benefits, but the Adonis emerging from the car cut her short.

Elegant masculine expensive shoes appeared as the door of the Lamborghini flew open, followed by strong powerful legs clad in impeccable designer jeans which clung to the swell of his muscular thighs. A merlot-pink cotton shirt hugged his toned pecs, complimenting his olive skin and tanned face.

As he strode from the car with the commanding gait that designated him the world's reigning alpha, Lily took a labored, shallow breath from her chest. She gripped the steering wheel as she braced herself for what was sure to be a torrent of anger—then changed her mind.

Flinging her door open she got out to head him off. The last thing she wanted was to be trapped in a confined space with no way out; no way to protect herself; nowhere to run.

Suddenly, without warning, the anger exploded in her chest, and this far too good looking hunk, this rich stupid man, who thought himself superior, was her target.

"What the hell were you doing," she hissed at him. She glared at the tall, dark and handsome man's chiseled cheek-bones and golden-toned skin. *Life's definitely been easy for you.* "You braked without warning. I could have been killed."

He stared at her with blank, slack-jawed, amusement. "You're right. I'm sorry. How inconsiderate of me. I should have run over the kid's dog."

Dog? What dog? She hadn't seen a dog.

"You never indicated!" Lily knew she was raving but she couldn't stop. "Why didn't you put your hand out the window to warn me?" Lily turned to Ernesto. "You should have made him indicate!' Her voice rose beyond the bounds of what was acceptable in a public place.

A bemused smile grazed his formidable lips. His gaze met hers in a moment of recognition, then flickered like a silent movie into darkness.

Did she know him? He looked familiar? A gnawing sense of déjà vu collided with the torrent of anger and fear surging through her body in a maelstrom of opposing currents.

As his cool stare assessed her, sliding down the length of her flowery, flowing maxi dress, at last he spoke.

"You're the counselor!" he shouted.

5

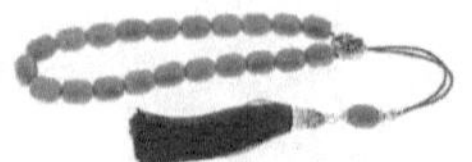

"**I**'m not a counselor," Lily said, realization sinking in. *Not anymore,* she said, silently. She sucked in a deep breath as a wave of nausea swept through her gut.

Any moment she would puke and the last thing she wanted to do was vomit all over his expensive calf-skin shoes.

Run! An inner voice commanded.

So she booted it, as best she could in a kaftan dress that wrapped around her ankles as she sprinted through the crowded streets.

Suddenly strong arms encircled her waist. She felt the warmth and strength of his touch as his hands encircled her belly. She sensed his calm, steady demeanor. She intuited no anger or hostility or danger. She had a craven urge to cling to him, but the behavior that had driven him to seize her made it inappropriate.

Badly inappropriate. Didn't he realize that?

She had fled the scene of an accident. She had shirked her responsibilities. She had done the unthinkable. She was an experienced counselor, *his counselor*—she was supposed to have her shit together.

"Let me go," she said in deliberate dismissal.

But he felt so strong and powerful. A rock to lean on and Lily ached for the support that his protection seemed to offer.

Hold me and never let me go, she thought, noticing the kick of disappointment as he released his grip.

She felt sick and excited; afraid and exhilarated; guilty and rebellious. Every conflicting emotion collided through her body, reducing her to a quivering mess.

She wanted to be independent—she dreamed of someone to rely on.

She wanted to be alone—she dreamed of sharing her life.

She wanted—

She closed her eyes and clenched them shut. God, she didn't know what she wanted anymore. All she knew was she never wanted to hurt like she had years ago when the bad boy billionaire she'd once trusted with her future did a runner.

She was a mess, Lily affirmed, as she registered the crowd gathered around them. *And the whole tiny town knew it.*

"*Mia moglie*, my wife," Leonardo said to the swelling number of onlookers. "We like to play catch."

Wife?

Okay, to be honest, the first time he walked inside her counseling room she thought Roman gods really did walk the earth. She dreamt one day she could marry a man as hand-some and charismatic as Leonardo Ermenegildo Bressolini. She knew if she did, she sure as hell wouldn't cheat on him like his own wife had. She also knew that poor-town girls like her didn't marry uptown boys.

Was it his money, his good looks, or the security a life with him promised that made her insides churn into warm gooey fudge? Ans was it the fear of shattered dreams that made these reckless feelings quickly harden until they stabbed her insides like brittle toffee?

Conscious of the crowd pressing around her Lily's heart quickened as she scanned the familiar faces. Max and his wife Tina had stepped out of the cafe they managed to witness the commotion outside. They bent their heads together and whispered and pointed in her direction. Brian, from the bookstore, crossed his arms and frowned. One of the kids she had counseled stood, mouth gaping. A middle-aged man's body grew hard and tense as he looked, and he passed quickly by.

Dread wormed through her. Her life was over.

"Okay feeding time at the zoo is over," Leonardo said, his strong brow furrowing. His thick mane of hair, and golden-toned skin, and the fierce authority of his voice reminded Lily of a lion, as he swept his powerful hands toward the crowd. Her eyes stung. He was the king of the jungle with his majestic stance, his fear striking roar and his undeniable quest to protect her from pain.

"Go on. Showtime is finished," he growled, fixing the last of the rubberneckers with a savage look that sent them fleeing.

"*Scusa, è colpa mia,*" he said, returning to her side. "I'm sorry, this is my fault. I created a spectacle." His thick, sultry Italian accent lingered on her tastebuds like treacle.

Part of Lily's mind registered his earnest concern and caring. But then fear kicked in. When something goes right it only gets taken away, she thought. Good things don't happen to kind people. Billionaires don't rescue paupers.

"No, it's my fault. I shouldn't have run. My following distance—it wasn't what it should be. I'll take responsibility of course. I will pay, somehow." Somehow being the operative word she thought as he turned around and looked toward her heap of a car in the distance. "I panicked." Just like I panic every time I think of a future with no way to pay her bills, she mused.

She fiddled with her fingers as she turned back to him.

"Would you consider installments?"

* * *

While Leonardo didn't respect people who tried to escape their responsibilities, there was something about this wild creature racing away that stimulated his curiosity.

Most of the women he met, and all the ones he bedded, were compliant, subservient, irritatingly meek. Something about her spontaneous flight excited him—but also incited caution.

What had made her flee? He had not been overly harsh, he had held back his anger. While he was renown for his strength, his ruthlessness, and his complete command of the world around him, he rarely unleashed his wrath on women.

Bar one—that horrid lady from the adoption agency who had treated him so despicably.

But he had raised his voice to the enchanting vixon as she fled, and he regretted that. Clearly, he had startled the counselor as much as he had been startled by her dramatic collision into his life.

"You dropped these," he said, reaching into his pocket for the string of Carnelian stones that had fallen from her hands as she fled.

Worry beads.

He recognized their purpose immediately. Judging from the dilapidated condition of her car clearly she had a lot to worry about—not least of which was how exactly she was going to pay for the damage she'd done to his Lamborghini.

His fingers ran over the smooth surface of the rich dark red beads she had fondled repeatedly, sending a frisson of fire zinging through his body. The flames of desire licked their heated temptation over parts of him that had never felt anything in years. It was as disconcerting as it was worrying.

More worryingly he had called her his wife.

Perhaps he should hang onto the beads, he thought momentarily.

He had cultivated his reputation as a stone-hearted bastard for a reason. Staying rigid kept his demons at bay. the counselor was a do-gooder, and if she was like any of the other do-gooders who had paraded through his life, she was more damaged than he was. And quite possibly, as much of a manufacturer of truth as they had all been, too. Hadn't they all lied to him? At least she'd been honest enough to flee, he thought, amused at the irony.

He handed her the beads which she readily grasped as if he were handing her a life raft in a dangerous sea. Her face was pale, luminous, beautiful.

She clutched the worry beads to her chest. She was probably wondering, how the hell was she going to get out of this mess?

His dark brows curved into a frown, not the frown of an angry man, but a man perplexed by the hapless woman in front of him and the feelings she stirred.

He felt protective but also smitten. Hadn't he always seen himself a protector of those most vulnerable?

Si. And that was exactly what got him into trouble. Danger. Danger. Danger, the bell tolled, and yet he refused to listen.

Suddenly he felt his appetite for recklessness deepen. She was as dangerous as the engulfing seas that ravaged the rocks beneath his impenetrable luxury retreat. Yet she was also in need. And the truth was he needed her as much as she needed him.

"You will work for me," he said, with uncharacteristic spontaneity.

She said nothing, just stared at him, her face red and scowling.

What the hell had come over him? He was in need of a housekeeper, not a bewitchingly wild and reluctant siren.

"You will work off the debt." He kept his voice deliberately hard, just as he intended to keep his heart—rigid, frozen, and totally ice on the rocks. "I am a man in want of a keeper," he said, before he had the chance to correct the terms of her engagement. "It's a live-in position."

He glanced at the beads clutched in her hand which seemed to pulse with excitement at his decision.

Would he regret inviting her into his life?

6

L ily didn't want a Cinderella rescue. She wanted to maintain her independence and do something meaningful with her life.

But for now, perhaps it was time to let the old ways die. Besides, what choice did she have? Besides, it wasn't as if she wouldn't be earning her keep.

"I'll accept your offer but only until I am back on my financial feet. And only on several conditions. The first, I won't be your lover."

If he is a pimp, she thought, that will clear any misunderstandings. For all she knew he wanted her to make beds in an upmarket bordello for rich and bored billionaires who had nothing better to do with their time and money.

"And the second," she said, injecting her voice with sufficient business propriety, "I need my own space."

"I can assure you that I have never had to pay a woman to sleep with me. You may make my bed, but you may not lie in it," Leonardo said, derisively.

"That's fine by me," Lily said, noticing a spike of indignation in her voice. She would make herself busy. If his fancy car was anything to go by he'd live in something palatial with loads of rooms that needed cleaning. It was honest work, and it would keep her mind off the betrayal at work.

It was time to say 'yes' to a new door opening, and 'no' to the one now firmly shut. She was being led, she just didn't know where or why. And for some absurd reason, it felt right.

If only she'd trusted her gut the first time she'd met Lying Lavina.

She stole a glance at Leonardo who was staring intensely at her hands. She followed his gaze and noticed with embarrassment her fingers had been running a brisk pace across her beads.

"They're carnelian crystals," she said, then added "an action stone, one that reminds me to be, 'in the moment.'"

He looked bemused. "Perhaps, if you'd been more in the now, you wouldn't have collided with my Lamborghini. However, now that you are in the moment, and imbued with all that action energy, it's time to get to work. My employee will drive your—" his brow frowned as though digesting something unpalatable. "You will drive with me."

"Don't you trust me?"

"No, *mia cara* I don't."

7

"How rude," she said as she climbed into the car of dreams. Despite her annoyance, she smiled to herself, relishing in the taste of those harsh words as much as the comfort of the plush cream leather seat beneath her bum.

For the first time, she didn't care about being a people pleaser, or whether he liked her, She had supreme luxury in sight and she was going to run with it.

She would be his housekeeper, not his slave, and she would begin as she meant to continue. She would speak her mind. She liked that he seemed to appreciate her forthrightness.

"Rude—yet truthful," Leonardo said. "You crashed into

my car and ran. I had to chase after you. You resisted—what part of trust have I missed?"

Lily felt herself smile again and pressed her lips shut. Nope, looking like you enjoyed something only invited trouble, she reminded herself, recalling the mistake she had made telling Lying Lavina how much she loved her job. She ended up looking like a naive fool and a victim.

"I panicked—for all I know you could have lost control and hit me."

"Hit you?" he pulled the car over to the side of the road. "You honestly believe that?"

She looked down at her lap. "No," she said, quietly. "No, I don't. Of course, I don't...I wouldn't have got into your car and I wouldn't have accepted your offer...it's just..."

"Just what."

"Nothing," she said, wringing the beads in her hands.

Suddenly he placed a warm, protective palm over hers. "You'll be safe at *Casa dei Sogni*. No one will harm you there."

Whether it was the softness of his touch or his words imbued with such knowing and understanding, she didn't know. All she knew was that she had to stop the tears welling in her eyes from falling.

Cry baby she was not. Soft touch she was no longer. Naive she would never be again.

She moved her hand from beneath his, instantly wishing it could remain there forever.

"I just want to do my job. I just want to pay my debt. I just want to get on with my life." She looked out the window, as they entered Pahia, the gateway to the mesmerizing Bay of Islands.

"Are we there yet?" she asked, as they wound their way

along the slinky road which hugged the golden sandy beaches and the shimmering Pacific Ocean.

She loved that people pointed and stared at the car as they drove by. The truth was she wanted to drive with Leonardo forever. She felt like a queen.

"Soon, *mia cara*." Leonardo said.

His cultivated Italian accent rang every alarm bell in Lily's body. The feeling was as nice as it was unsettling.

They drove another 15-minutes toward the car ferry at Opua, and she filled in the silence as they made the crossing. Lily told him how she'd made her prayer beads herself and how she loved everything to do with crystals. And she was pleased to find he actually, genuinely, honestly listened. It was refreshing. She was used to being the listener. It was rare for anyone to return the considerate attention she so freely gave.

And then she did something she almost never did. Not with strangers, anyway. She shared with him her belief that crystals have magical healing powers and that they do this by positively interacting with your body's energy field, or chakra.

He didn't ridicule her. He didn't ask for the scientific evidence. He didn't accuse her of manufacturing snake oil like some people had. His quiet acceptance was as surprising as it was comforting.

They continued talking for the twenty minutes it took from leaving the ferry to arriving at their final destination. He told her about his water empire and she couldn't believe how much money came from something bestowed so liberally from the heavens. She couldn't help but be impressed when he told her of all the charities and community organizations where he donated money.

Despite her formidable attempts not to like him she felt a

huge amount of respect. Respect was safe. You couldn't get your heart torn out of your chest if you respected someone, could you? It wasn't dangerous, like loving, was it?

Leonardo remained oblivious to Lily's ricocheting thoughts as at last he pulled off the road, and turned into an immaculately landscaped drive on a steep incline. He stopped short of the two towering thick gold gates blocking the entry, flanked on either side by two winged lions.

He entered his pin code into the security system and waited to be granted entry.

Gosh, it was exciting.

"Welcome to *Casa dei Sogni*. House of Dreams," he said, as the gates slid back, revealing a world Lily never thought in her wildest dreams she would ever see.

It was too good to be true.

8

L ily pinched her arm. "Are you for real?"

Car of dreams. House of dreams. Man of dreams. It just didn't seem conceivable. She had rubbed her carnelian crystal beads and they had delivered big time.

She had set her intention that she'd like to fight like a warrior, play matriarch and say what she damned well pleased—for once.

Tick. Done that.

She had asked that just for once she'd like to have someone by her side helping her slay the demons and monsters masquerading as nice people.

Half tick. So far he hadn't been a monster.

She had prayed that just for once she'd like someone to love her unconditionally—forever and always.

Quarter tick. He hadn't made her feel like a weirdo about her crystals or laughed at the words, 'I'm Following My Passion, Are You?' emblazoned on her car. So far, he'd accepted her unconditionally. It was a quarter tick, but miles ahead of anything she had ever experienced from anyone in her life.

Anytime soon a genie was going to pop out of some bottle she had yet to unearth and tell her she had been punked. Good things didn't happen to her. This had to be some sick practical joke, sprung on her by a reality show.

She looked around for the camera crew, but only saw paradise.

Palm trees swayed in the gentle breeze, seemingly in sync to the rhythm of the music playing softly along the path which led to another gated entrance.

Passing through the palest of milky-white painted plaster walls, the faint aroma of geranium came into focus. Lily's breath slowed then deepened.

Was that sandalwood she could smell, and a hint of orange, too? Her gaze fluttered to the seashell pink hibiscus, the flower of happiness and sheer joy, with honeyed nectar that tasted so sweet on the lips.

As Lily gazed at the tumble of bougainvillea flopping over the low plaster wall she imagined what it would feel like to know this home was yours forever, always ready to begin your blissful journey at a place where gentility and luxury are a matter of course. Delights awaited—for those lucky enough to legitimately call *Casa dei Sogni* their house of dreams.

She sighed despondently. Lily was the hired help and she may as well accept it. Of course, she was grateful. Who wouldn't be? But she would not allow herself to become delusional.

She glanced at Leonardo as they entered an arched covered walkway that led to the main house. Gosh, he was hot. Almost as hot as the searing pink walls of the tunnel he guided her through.

Too bad, she'd would never taste the sweet, sultry nectar of his kisses. Good grief, she thought, wiping beads of sweat from her brows. She must need her head examined. He would no sooner want to kiss her than he would suck the face of a frog. He was strictly a top-shelf kind of guy, not a bottom dweller who swept the ocean floor mopping up cast offs. The sooner she accepted the reality of her position the better they'd all get along.

"What happened to your car?" a man asked, stepping from the garden.

"She happened to my car," Leonardo said, gesturing to Lily.

Lily felt her face burn. It was only the fact that a slight grin lay beneath Leonardo's scowl that stopped her from turning around and running.

"Lily…" He said turning to his friend. "*Scusi*, I don't remember your last name," Leonardo said, turning back to her. For a brief moment, his gaze locked with hers and her heart burned.

"Lily Rose," she stuttered.

"Si. I remember. You have a beautiful name—just like the face of the lady who claims it."

Lily felt her blush deepen four-fold. *Liar.* But she liked the compliment anyway.

"Lily Rose, meet Tomasso Rivetti. He and his wife Joey are staying with me for the weekend. They are winemakers— very good winemakers, too. Organic wine. Better than the wine I produce here," he said, sweeping his hand to the left where a tangle of vines ran up the steep hillside.

"Enchanted," Tomasso said, taking her hand and kissing it.

A girl could get used to this, Lily thought briefly before reminding herself that men of formidable wealth had triple degrees in charm school. Still, they meant no harm. All she had to do was stay grounded.

"Tomasso and Joey are staying in Skyfall."

"Skyfall?"

Grounded. Grounded. Grounded, she affirmed to herself.

"Come, I will show you," Leonardo said, as they reached the house.

Lily gasped as he opened the floor to ceiling paneled wooden doors, revealing an unspoiled billionaire's view of the ocean.

She held her breath as they wound through the house out to the outside decks, past antiques and curios, marble sculptures and a grand piano fit for Liberace.

The whole house was a riot of clashing patterns and color. But it worked in a way that only the Italians could pull off. Judging from the decor, she thought, her gaze drifting across the cobwebs and the layer of dust that coated everything, Leonardo was as eccentric as he was rich.

She liked that. No, she loved that. The house screamed, 'creative' and 'fun'. She never would have picked it, she thought glancing at Leonardo. He'd been so repressed and stiff in the sessions she'd had with him and his wife. And sad.

But this place, well, it just seemed so happy. Clearly, it was his happy place. His retreat from the madness of the world. She could relate to that. Definitely.

And the view. Man. The view. It literally took her breath away. She stood stunned, unable to comprehend that vastness of the ocean which glittered like diamonds and the incalculable wealth that had afforded such a majestic piece of paradise.

It was so hypnotic that is was easy not to think of the alluring archipelago of 144 islands that stretched beyond the azure sea in a view that whispered infinity. And for a moment, she forgot all her troubles.

Lily had never dreamed that a car crash that wiped out her bank account could turn into one of the best days of her life.

"I did die in that crash," she said, turning to Leonardo. "I died and drove to heaven."

And as she glanced up into the dark, infinite eyes of the man who had offered her a haven from poverty; the man she had first met so intimately during his therapy sessions; the man who now stood so heroically at her side, her eyes met his in a flame of deep recognition.

Though she knew that while, for now, she was the hired help, she sensed that Cinderella had found her prince, and he would help her create the life she always dreamed of. But sweetest of all, she knew they would be together forever and always.

* * * THE END * * *

AUTHOR'S NOTE

I can relate to Danielle Steele who says to always be on guard against envy. "Envy is a very ugly thing and very dangerous. You have to protect yourself from it every day."

As with all my stories, *Forever and Always*, was sparked by a true event, or rather several true events.

I started to write this short story following a toxic work experience. It's a love story—so of course, it had to have a happy ending.

As the opening quote of this book suggests, sometimes the worst of times can turn out to be blessings in disguise.

As I type this note, I am vacationing in Turks and Caicos, in the Caribbean—voted the most beautiful island in the world. Earlier in the year I began this story while holidaying in American Samoa. If these terrible things had not happened to me back in 2018, I doubt I would have visited paradise —twice.

Whatever troubles have dogged you or you are facing now, open your heart and you will see how blessed you are to have these events, people, or setbacks in your life. Sometimes they are the light that shines your path through some dark phases of life toward a better life. Never lose hope.

THIS SHORT STORY is a prequel to a magical new series, *Seven Stars*—seven spell-binding stories of heartbreak, family, destiny and unconditional love.

FOREVER AND ALWAYS IS NOW AVAILABLE as an audiobook for your listening enjoyment. Check out a free sample or grab your copy from your favorite online retailer.

SIGN up for my newsletter and be the first to know when books in the *Seven Stars* series are released.

But right now, I'm so excited to tell you about about book two in the Passion Down Under Sassy Short Stories collection, and to gift you a FREE copy of book one. I hope you love them, as much as I adored writing them.

P.S.

If you'd like to learn more about these characters, gain inside tips into the writing process, or be the first to know when a new book is released, subscribe to my newsletter here: http://eepurl.com/cigEsH. Please email me and I'll be in touch personally—I promise…mollie@molliemathews.com.

ACKNOWLEDGMENTS

My sincere thanks to my beta readers who picked up a few plot inconsistencies in the first edition and graciously agreed to check my revised version.

Firstly I'd like to thank JoAnne Weiss. Not only was she one of the first reader of my beta copy of Forever and Always, but she also provided the most amazing editing and proofreading sweep of the book, which I truly appreciated. I'm not the last author to admit that this is not a strong point. But I know that getting the detail right is so important and impacts how we enjoy reading.

Elaine Zieroth, I love the level of detail she went into and I truly appreciate her willingness to help me improve. What she calls her pickiness is actually her superpower. You spot things others miss, bring tremendous humor to the editing process and you have been a great cheerleader. I am honored that in your retirement years you have taken my talent under your wing to nurture.

I am truly indebted.

And yes, chocolate was a great idea—I devoured three chocolate biscuits with a cup of tea as I worked through the edits. Who needs an excuse, right!

My sincere thanks also to hi Pat thank you so much for your feedback I really appreciate it and those lovely words to here as well

To the love of my life, Lorenzo, thank you for blessing me with this extraordinary life. Your passion and perseverance inspires me.

And lastly, but importantly, thank you to my family who have been supporting my daughter Hannah during some extremely difficult times while I have been overseas. I shall love you forever and always.

BOOK TWO IN THE SERIES OUT NOW!

Did you enjoy reading this short story?
Book One and Two in the Passion Down Under Sassy Short
Stories *series available now:*
Twist of Fate
Love me Forever

Met Leonardo's winemaking friends Tomasso Rivetti and
Viticulturist Joey Harper. Discover how they met and journey
with them as they fall in love.

Sometimes the end is just the beginning...

Viticulturist Joey Harper's organic vineyard is under siege
from neighboring landowners with chemical sprays, wanting
to turn a fast profit, and someone purchasing large tracts of
land under incredible secrecy.
But Joey's not someone who dwells on her own troubles. She
has only one wish—following the still-birth of her sister's
first child, she prays her much loved younger sister may
conceive again.

Using her inherited gift for magic, she enlists the aid of the
ancient walnut tree which towers majestically over her
organic vineyard. What she doesn't realize is that her one
wish, begets another, and her unselfish desire for her sister's
happiness send's love to her—in the form of a most
unsuitable and irresistible admirer.

Venetian winemaking tycoon Tomasso Rivetti has it all: a loving family, good looks, and a considerable fortune. When he ventures Down Under to New Zealand, underneath his apparently perfect world, cracks begin to appear…and no one is more surprised than Tomasso when the billionaire lifestyle he takes for granted is turned upside down by a chance encounter.

But despite Tomasso's determined pursuit of Joey's affection, her broken heart remains closed—to protect herself and her vineyard from a terrible threat.
Distance keeps her safe. But as a final battle draws close, Joey and Tomasso are drawn irresistibly together. And while they succumb to the heat between them, they both know there can be no tomorrow…

If you enjoy stories with a touch of magic and fantasy and with that so important happy ending, you'll love this powerful new love story.

"Tugs at the heartstrings."

"I love Mollie Mathews."

"Heart-warming and beautiful with passion."

"*Love Me Forever* has a lovely mystical feel about it, with deep longings being experienced by the characters."

Available now!

THANK YOU

Thank you for reading *Forever and Always…* I hope you loved it. If you did…

1. Help other people find this book by writing a review
2. Signup for my new releases email to find out about the next book as soon as I release it, sign up here http://eepurl.com/ghM501
3. Email me at mollie@molliemathews.com with a copy of your honest review and let me know if you'd love to join my dream team and of advance readers
4. Follow me on BookBub, https://www.bookbub.com/authors/mollie-mathews
5. Stay in touch on Facebook, https://www.facebook.com/molliemathewsnz
6. Follow me on Twitter - https://twitter.com/Molliemathewsnz
7. Be inspired on Pinterest - https://nz.pinterest.com/

molliemathews and Instagram - https://www.
instagram.com/molliemathewsauthor
8. Follow my blog - https://molliemathews.
wordpress.com

Read on for a sneak peek into Mollie's full-length books, *Married by Christmas* and *Flight of Passion, and Claimed By The Sheikh.*

But first, enjoy the first book in the Passion Down Under Sassy Short Stories, series Twist of Fate, Absolutely FREE!

TWIST OF FATE

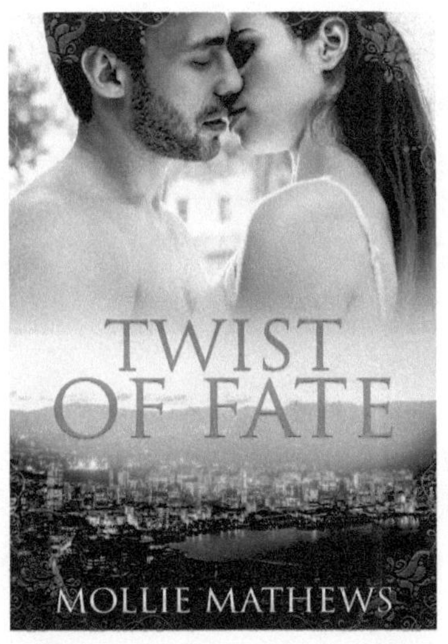

What if a twist of fate could change your life?

Still reeling following his unexpected divorce, billionaire Tech guru Jonathan James has returned home feeling disillusioned and low in spirits. The last thing he needs when he flies home from London to New Zealand is complications.

When a baggage mix up leaves him with nothing but a suitcase full of stilettos, lush lashes and Dolly Parton-like wigs, he goes in search of the owner. He quickly discovers that all is not as it seems as his life takes off in a hilarious and unexpected direction.

A Twist of Fate is a short story full of quirky humor and the promise of romance.

Set in Wellington, New Zealand—the coolest little capital in the world.

FOREWORD

Dear Friends,

I hope you enjoy *Twist of Fate*. It's a love story close to my heart and touches on a number of subjects I love and care about with the twists and turns in the plot. I always love celebrating the strength of the human spirit, and how unexpected events can change our lives for the better.

Love comes in many forms and colors and is an exciting, fascinating and rewarding victory if we listen to the whispers of our soul, and are willing to open our hearts and take a chance on finding ever-lasting happiness again.

In part, this story was inspired by a chance encounter with a wonderful and generous man during a very stressful time when I was stuck in an airport queue. I had just flown from New York to LA and it looked like I would miss my flight. Long story short, Jonathan—a wealthy derivatives dealer from New York, was flying to my hometown, Wellington, New Zealand.

He offered to give up his first-class seat so that I could make my flight. We became great friends and I invited him to have dinner with my family. I found out that night, as he played on my mom's piano and my daughter accompanied him on vocals, that he was an uber-talented jazz pianist.

Jonathan sent me CD's of his favorite jazz music from New York, including the one I mention in this story. And later he invited my daughter and I to stay with him and his new girlfriend, Danni (with an *i*)—a former Broadway dancer, in New York. I loved learning about their love story. And this sparked the seeds of this romantic tale.

But there is another reason I decided to write this story. "To keep your joy alive sometimes you need to write something just for the fun of it. This keeps your writing chops sharp and your writer's soul soaring," says thriller writer, James Scott Bell.

That's how it was with my short story *Twist of Fate*. It's not my usual romance or beat, but it was a story I wanted to write. It makes me happy that it's out there— and that readers like you have found it.

With all my love,
Mollie

1

"How are you, mate?'" Mac asked Jonathan James, as he pulled up to the curb outside Wellington's domestic airport.

Jonathan gave Mac a weary smile, as his best friend hopped out of his Land Rover. "I've been better. That London flight was grueling."

"That's not what I meant."

"I know. What can I say? Jacinda wanted out of the marriage and nothing I said, nothing I tried, nothing I promised her would change her mind."

"She always was a selfish cow," Mac said.

Jonathan glanced up at the gray, broody sky. New Zealand's capital city, true to nature, had turned out a particularly bleak and desolate day.

"It's good to be back home." At least some things never changed.

As he reached for the handle of his suitcase, a sudden gust of Wellington's infamous wind spun it around, sending it veering off the curb.

"What the hell!" Mac exclaimed as the suitcase flew

open, spilling the contents onto the road. Long blonde wigs, corsets, high-heeled stilettos, false eyelashes, makeup, and books spewed out of the case and lay in a tangled heap.

A couple of kids rigged out in the latest rapper clothing, bling swinging from their necks and black hoodies shielding their heads, raised their eyebrows and wolf-whistled as they walked past.

"Jeez, Jonny, what's happened to you since you've been in London?" Mac said, picking up one of the books, as Jonathan scrambled to gather the strange belongings.

"There can be no culture without the drag queen," Mac said, reading out loud. "Is there something you're not telling me? Is that why the cow threw you out?"

"That's not my book and that's not my suitcase. I may be open-minded, but I'm no queen."

Mac ran his hand over his designer stubbled chin and looked dubiously at his best mate. Even though he hadn't seen Jonny for more than nine years, as far as he recalled he didn't have a penchant for wearing women's clothes. "Whose case is it then?"

"I must've picked up the wrong bag," Jonathan cursed, as he bent down and read the luggage tag. "Danny Zouski."

"Who the hell's Danny Zouski?" Mac asked.

"Damn! I bet ya that guy's got my luggage," Jonathan said, sweeping his hand through his thick mop of black wavy hair.

"Danny sounds like an interesting character. What sort of dude gets around in this?" Mac held up a pink silk bodice with black frilly lace and white satin ribbon, and in his other hand, he raised a pair of pink fishnets. "Give me a kiss, sugar," he joked, putting on a blonde Dolly Parton-like wig.

"Idiot," Jonathan laughed, swiping Mac playfully. "Somewhere this guy Danny's got my stuff and I want it back." He grabbed his iPhone from his jacket pocket and punched in the number he found on the luggage tag.

"Hello? Is this Danny Zouski?...You're who? Danny's tied up?" Jonathan quirked his thick brows. "Kinky," he whispered as he winked at Mac. "

"Look, there's been a mix-up. I have Danny's suitcase... sure I'll wait....yeah, I'm Jonathan. You've got my bag?... That's great...Look, can you tell me how to get to you? Yeah, yeah, we'll bring the bags over... sure, no sweat, we can get there in time."

"What's going on?"

"The good news is that Danny has my gear. Apparently, he's in some sort of show in town."

"What kind of show?" Mac asked suspiciously, holding a pair of crotchless knickers.

"Dunno," Jonathan said, bunching everything into the suitcase and hauling it into the back of the Range Rover. "All I know is we've got to get this gear to him quick."

2

"Do you want me to come in with you for protection… just in case?" Mac joked as they pulled up outside the back entrance of the St James Theatre. "This guy Danny might fancy you. You are kind of cute, Jonny boy."

"Get out of here! This'll just take a minute. I'll give the stuff to Danny, get my bag, and get the hell out of there."

Jonathan jumped out of the car and knocked on the giant, worn door. A bulky guy dressed in a skin-tight pink T- shirt and green leggings that clung to his private bits, in all the wrong ways, stepped outside.

"I'm here to see Danny," Jonathan said.

"Is Danny expecting you?" the bulky guy asked, folding his arms and frowning.

"Yep, he's got something for me."

"Is that right?" he said, raising his eyebrows. "Okay, pretty boy, in you go. Take the first right door, then left, and on your right again. Name's on the door."

Jonathan stepped out of the sunlight and into a dark narrow passage. He looked briefly down at the black suitcase. It looked the same, yet its contents were nothing like his own.

He'd deliberately traveled light, leaving behind the memories of his married life in London, ready to start again.

He bit back a curse as he rubbed his chest, where everything felt tight. He was fit, a powerhouse of strength, but it still hurt like the devil to have failed at marriage.

He dragged the case along the dark corridors that wove through the old theatre and stopped in front of a door with a brass plate and a gold star beside it, which read 'Danny Zouski.' Jonathan shifted uncomfortably as he waited for his knock to be answered.

"What do you want?" purred a soft voice that oozed sensuality.

And femininity.

"Danny?" he asked tentatively. "You're a *she*," he said, regretting the stupid comment as soon as the words slipped from his mouth, as the woman behind the voice opened the door.

Wow! Danny-girl was a knock-out. The silk fabric of her pink robe clung to her shapely body, accentuating all her curves—in exactly the right places.

Bright-pink platform shoes gave her small frame a flattering lift, adding length to her shapely legs and drawing his eyes towards her face.

Her black eyes sparkled mischievously, as though reveling in his shock.

She had no make-up on and in that moment Jonathan thought she was the most beautiful woman he had ever seen.

"Danny with a 'y'—I thought girls spelled it with an 'i,'" he tried to explain.

"I like the 'y'," she said. "'Y' for why should I follow the crowd. 'y' for why be dependent on others. 'y' for why should I be like other women, and 'y' because *why are you so darned cute!*"

"Really?"

"Kind of," she said, blushing. "My dad was hoping for a boy, and he spelled it that way." As she bent to check the label on her case the robe fell open lightly, providing a glimpse of her creamy white cleavage.

"You're a lifesaver," she whispered in a sultry voice that ricocheted through his chest. She stood on her tiptoes, drawing herself up to meet his 6ft 3-inch frame and kissed him.

Jonathan almost fainted.

3

———

"**I** go on in 30 minutes," Danny said, oblivious to the fireworks in Jonathan's loins and the longing in his heart.

"Everything I need is in that case—my wig, my lashes, the books I've been reading to help me with my new part." She reached out, her fingers brushing his as she grabbed the handle of her case.

"I'll swap you," she smiled, her fingers wrapping over his momentarily, before pulling away. Jonathan noticed a slight flush of pink color on her cheeks.

"You travel light, don't you?" she said, wheeling his suitcase toward him. "Jeans and tee-shirts, that's all you've got— are you running away or something?"

"Ah... um." For once in his life Jonathan was speechless. How could he even begin to explain the torture of the last few years?

"Oh, where are my manners? Leaving you standing out there in that musty old hall like that. Come in. Come in."

"You're busy, I should get going," he said, recovering his voice.

"You couldn't' stick around, could you? The truth is, I hate being alone before a show. I get so nervous. I'd be glad of the company—and the distraction," she said, smiling.

Something about the way her eyes lit up the room, something about the way her smile danced on her lips, something about the way his heart skipped—despite his vow to never get involved with women again—made the choice easy.

"Sure."

4

"What do you feel like listening to?" she called out, reaching for her makeup as Jonathan made a quick call and told Mac to go ahead without him. "I'm a jazz fan myself."

"No way!" Jonathan said, snapping the phone shut."Me too!" What were the odds? He couldn't believe his luck. A girl who loved jazz as much as he did. His wife—ex-wife, he corrected himself, hated jazz. She hated music. She hated noise—and, as it turned out she hated him.

'This is my favorite track," she said, pushing play on the iPod docked on her make-up table. "The Keith Jarrett Trio. Do you know them?"

"Know them? Are you kidding? I love them! Don't tell me...this is... let me see..." he said, trying to recall where he'd heard the tune before. "I know, it's from their album, *Standards in Norway*."

"Hey, you're pretty good," she giggled. "How come you know so much?" she said, troweling on a layer of iridescent blue eyeshadow. She leaned toward the mirror and carefully placed lush false lashes, edged with diamantes, on her lids, then swept her lips with a wave of glossy fuchsia pink.

"I trained as a jazz pianist," Jonathan said, wanting to tell her she didn't need makeup to have the wow factor. "I grew up on the stuff. But it's been a while." Too long, he thought. Awareness dawning as the dulcet tones of the jazz wove their magic around them.

Far too long.

The relentless hours he'd spent amassing considerable wealth and a formidable reputation as a tech tycoon left little room for passion.

"That's so cool!" she said, slipping behind a screen, and emerging minutes later, in a shimmering blue sequin skin hugging dress. She turned around and backed toward him.

"Can you zip me up?"

Jonathan's pulse soared as his fingers clasped the end of the zipper where it rested just above her tailbone, as he drew it slowly along the length of her lithe body.

"My father's a sax player," Danny said, bunching her shoulder-length flaxen hair, into a pile on top of her head. "All my life has been spent around musicians...and the theatre. My mom's an actress," she said, taking the Dolly Parton-like wig from her case and tugging it onto her head.

"How do I look?" she said, dropping her voice to a husky male-like tone. "Over the top enough?"

Jonathan's gaze lingered over her breasts, popping over the edge of her dress, for longer than was polite. But then she did ask. "Yip, plenty over the top," he said playfully. "You look like a pro!'"

Except she wasn't a pro, not in the way he was used to. The sort of pro like his ex-wife who knew how to feign affection, who knew how to make a profession out of being disingenuous and disloyal. Who knew how, in one deft legal maneuver, to slice a huge chunk of his fortune and claim it as her own.

Instinct told Jonathan that Danny was no gold-digger, but one of the most sincere, honest, and fun-loving woman he had ever met. But experience told him to be cautious just the same.

The half-hour until the show flew as they chatted and listened to music. In a short period of time, he learned more about her, her hopes, dreams, and aspirations, than many of the people in his life. And she shared how excited she was to have been cast as one of the lead actresses in the musical 'Luna, Queen of the Drags.'

"It's a story about three incredible and highly competitive drag queens," Danny said, "Each of them is showcasing their considerably unique talents in a Clash of The Drag Queens at an Aussie resort amongst a swag of homophobic men. I love that it's fun and crazy and completely out there. It's how I would like to live my life. Not as a drag queen, but someone who's not afraid to live life more colorfully. And I like that in a small way, I'm helping educate people to have more tolerance and kindness towards others—despite our differences."

As Jonathan got up to leave, he realized the projection his ex-wife had hurled at him had been right. He'd never loved her. He never loved her coldness. He never loved her selfishness. He never loved the boring, quiet, soulless way she wanted them both to live their lives—amassing wealth and passing each other like ships on a cold, barren night.

But then she left him for a doubly boring, doubly selfish, doubly soulless, risk-averse investment banker. And now, with punching clarity, he knew that that suited him just fine.

LATER THAT NIGHT, as he watched Danny sing and dance her

way through the show, memories of his unhappy marriage disappeared.

Just when he'd thought he'd keep his heart cold, Danny had danced and sung her way into his life. For the first time, he was excited to see where fate would take them.

*** THE END ***

EXCERPT: MARRIED BY CHRISTMAS

MARRIED BY CHRISTMAS

What if the person who is so, so, so wrong for you is really so, so, so right, but you're too afraid to give love a chance?

Last Christmas art therapist Issy Riley was jilted by her fiancé. This Christmas she's running away. A week with a client on his private Fijian island promises to save her from cheating men and the London festive season. But when the client turns out to be a gorgeous and magnetic Italian billionaire, he threatens her resolve to never again trust her heart to the wrong man.

Milan fashion house leader and avowed bachelor Massimilliano Balforni has no intention of taking a vacation, despite his sister's insistence that he subject himself to an art therapy retreat following a minor heart attack. With an important collection due, he intends to fire his therapist and work, instead. But the determined and striking Issy gives his heart palpitations of a far more dangerous kind.

The one thing Max and Issy agree on: they are as wrong for each other as wrong gets. He's a workaholic playboy who believes emotion is a weakness. She's a romantic who yearns for a happily ever after.

As the tropical heat soars, they discover that in this battle between work and play, resistance only fuels attraction—and sometimes two wrongs make a very passionate right.

Set in two beautiful paradises—Milano, Italy and the tropical Pacific islands of Fiji.

(First published as The Italian Billionaire's Christmas Bride)

*One word frees us
of all the weight
and pain of life:
That word is love*
~ Sophocles

1

'*Che cavolo!* No! No! No! This will not do. Only an anorexic model could wear something that resembles a straw,' thundered Massimilliano Balforni, CEO of Emporio Balforni, Milan's most prestigious fashion house. His coal black brows knitted in a fierce line as he looked with disdain at the scatter of sketches the young designer splayed on Max's 15th Century walnut desk.

His protégé began to protest but one piercing look from the maestro forced his lips shut. His body stiffened as if frozen to the floor, reminded that his employer's wrath was more dangerous than black ice.

'Alexandria Gorbetz is a real woman, the world's richest woman, and someone like me that demands perfection.'

Max's mouth curved in a controlled smile. Was that fear he detected in the young man's face as Max pierced him with his dark gaze? He had every reason to be afraid. Enemies and friends alike knew Max had destroyed promising careers for lesser transgressions. Infinitesimal precision, extraordinary control, unrivaled beauty—Max suffered nothing less.

Pressing his fingertips to the smooth, cool parchment, he

paused momentarily as a childhood memory stirred in his consciousness. He sucked in a breath and swept his hands brusquely across the page. He was no longer the lonely child who furtively sketched movie stars in beautiful clothes and dreamed of a Hollywood life.

What was once an escape was now a thriving commercial enterprise with insatiable demands. Max flourished his gold fountain pen across the page, adding a sweep of curves to the hips and breasts of the bespoke wedding gown his fashion house had been commissioned to design.

Now at the helm of his multi-billion dollar empire Max was no longer a hands-on designer, but nothing went out the door without his final veto. Some called him a control freak and this he took not as a criticism but as the highest compliment.

He waited to feel the rush of joy he used to feel when drawing as a child. He stopped to await the all-consuming love that arose from knowing that no one possessed his raw talent and genius. He paused to feel the pride that came years later from knowing he designed dresses perfectly, to satisfy only one client on her most important day. There was nothing.

It shouldn't have surprised him. He had long ago accepted that he was unable to feel the joy that other people did. He'd turned off that part of himself years ago and had vowed never again to succumb to vulnerability. In its place, carefully groomed aloofness and instilling fear in others were traits he prized and relentlessly cultivated.

As his protégé braced for the consequences Max forced his thoughts back to the commission. While he felt nothing in his heart, what he did experience as he looked at the drawing of the wedding dress executed to his design was a coolly detached appreciation that satisfied the perfectionist in him.

The lines and structure now conformed absolutely to his definition of ideal. The controlled steel gray pallet reflected his personality and every detailed aspect had been meticulously executed as he had commanded. No randomness or chaos anywhere.

Having witnessed his parents' brutal marriage and subsequent divorce, Max had no misguided notions of happily-ever-after, nor any desire to marry.

Perfection in relationships was simply unattainable. But the knowledge that he was at the helm of an empire that created exquisite, extraordinarily elegant gowns admired by the world's most elite, at the same time preserving a historic tradition, filled him with a degree of pride.

But as for the rest of his life—the personal, emotional side—he felt nothing. And that suited him perfectly.

Max's long supple fingers drummed an impatient rhythm on the armrest of his chair. '*Allora*?' Well? People react to fear, not love, he reminded himself as he kept his voice soft, but somehow containing all the might of the towering spires of the Duomo looming beyond his window.

A slither of fear crept into the young designer's hushed apology. 'I should have thought more about the woman beneath the dress.'

'Thinking is not enough,' Max commanded, his voice a dark, stark thing in the quiet of his office. 'You must apply.' Taking the drawings in both hands he tore the pages down the middle. 'Begin again, and this time bring me excellence.'

Ignoring the tiny pin like tremors piercing his chest Max pushed back from the desk and rose to his feet as the young man retrieved the torn fragments and scuttled quickly toward the door. Striding across the room Max willed his racing heart to cede to his control.

2

―――――

'Calm yourself, please Maxie,' Sophia Balforni said, sweeping into his office she cast the young man a sympathetic look as their paths crossed. 'Have you thought about what I suggested?' she asked, gesturing to the art therapy brochure peeking from beneath a pile of contracts.

'I am surrounded by amateurs and now you want me to play like a child, *mia sorella*. I have never heard something so ridiculous.'

'You're my brother. The best brother in the world, but do you know what's holding you back? You're afraid of losing control. You're afraid that without all of this, she said, sweeping her hand around the room, 'you're worthless.'

'But all of this means nothing if you're dead. And none of this means anything without someone to share your heart and soul. I hope one day you're able to realize that you're wonderful for who you are, not just for what you've accomplished. But most of all I hope you're able to experience the unconditional love and support of someone who loves you for you.'

Max was neither given to excessive emotion nor impetuousness but his mood wrestled with his need for control. He threw open the shuttered windows of his office and inhaled the frigid Milano air with shallow, measured breaths.

He ran his hand over his broad chest, fingering momentarily the fine scar snaking across his heart. His mind had the endurance and stamina of one thousand oxen but two months ago his body had betrayed him.

His gaze swept down the Piazza then flew up the spires of the Duomo, dusted with snow and bejeweled in dazzling pre-Christmas lights as the cacophony of Vespas buzzed like irritated wasps through the open window.

Although he had always hated Christmas, he loved tradition and he loved the supreme elegance that the Milanese never failed to deliver, but it pained him to concede that never had his beloved city been so irritating. In fact, everything, and everyone was irritating. Even his designs bored him. He knew better than most that he must continually innovate or die. Grudgingly he accepted his sister was right. He needed to get away.

'I admit it's a little unconventional,' Sophia said, taking an assortment of pills and vitamins from a gold embossed pillbox and, after pouring a glass of mineral water into a crystal tumbler, she passed the pills and water to Max.

'Unconventional?' Max tossed the pills into his mouth, took a gulp of water and threw back his head, grimacing as they slid down his throat. 'What you are suggesting is childish.' *Childish*, isn't that exactly what his father had thrown in his face when, as a young boy, he'd first shown him his sketches. 'If this got out to my competitors,' he said, forcing his mind from a memory he vowed never to revisit, 'can you imagine what it would do to my reputation?'

'Not nearly as damaging as being paralyzed by a stroke and having to be spoon-fed, Sophia snapped. 'And since when have you cared what others think? Besides, you have an island on the other side of the world.

'One you've been too busy to visit. Fiji is remote enough for you to step away from the constant flash of cameras and be virtually anonymous,' she said, lowering her voice as Max's new PA cat-walked into his office. 'Call yourself Mr. Johnstone, or Mr. Smith, or whatever else you want, to protect your privacy.'

Beneath long-fringed lashes the PA gave Max a sultry look, trailing her gaze over his lean and muscled form, as she placed a collection of fashion magazines and media cuttings in a neat pile precisely as she'd been trained.

'Thank you, that will be all,' Sophia said, dismissing her.

'A nudist camp would be vastly more appealing,' Max's gaze trailed after his PA as she left his office. While he had no time for relationships, that didn't stop him from appreciating beauty. How much easier it would be to lie naked amongst a bevy of loveliness than expose his feelings to the spotlight.

Sophia rolled her eyes. 'I can just imagine what that would do to your blood pressure. Art, unlike making a career of intimately studying the curves of women, my dear brother, is therapeutic.'

'So you want me to go to kiddy school and make a fool of myself.' Irritation coursed through his veins as he ran his fingers around the neck of his shirt and loosened the starched white collar.

'You never had a childhood,' Sophia said, her voice almost a whisper. 'You grew up too fast. We both did. And now you're a thirty-five-year-old man who may not see forty.'

'I know you are trying to help but I told you I can handle it.' And he would. He would never abandon his responsibility. Unlike his father who had tried to combine work with marriage and failed at both, Max had gladly sacrificed his personal life for his career.

Abandoned at birth by his biological parents, raised briefly by strangers, then dumped in a boarding school, he had turned what could have been a weakness into his biggest strength.

Self-reliance.

'All this stress has engulfed you, Max. Only you can't see it. And it scares me. You've become a shell of yourself—more than you were already. A man so cut off from his feelings that you are devoid of emotion. You've become a lighthouse of a man—lonely in a crowd, aloof and detached. Uncaring.'

The words bounced off Max's chest like the final shards of Milan's winter sun reflecting off the panoramic glass windows. It was true. He no longer cared.

'What do you want from me, Sophia?'

She paused, concern pooling in her dark eyes. 'I want what our mother wants. I want you to be happy.'

His lips curved in a tight mocking smile. When had his real mother ever cared about his happiness? He knew what she really wanted. After suddenly reappearing in his life, she wanted a daughter-in-law and she wanted a grandson. Max shook his head and gave a short exacerbated sigh. She wanted the impossible.

He plunged his hand through his hair, raking it back from his brow. He should have had it cut razor short last week. Instead, he'd thrown himself into the roll out of his retail network of 60 Massimilliano Balforni boutiques and jewelry stores throughout China, and the pending development of his luxury hotel in Dubai, with such single-minded, unrelenting focus there had been no time for indulgences.

'I've done my research,' he said, adding his signed consent to the final contracts, 'and from every angle it all seems based on spurious psychology.' His hand closed around the pen as he looked up sharply.

Sophia sucked her breath as though steeling herself to battle with his formidable will. 'Unless you make some changes, and I mean massive changes,' Sophia glanced momentarily in the direction of Cimitero Maggiore, Milan's largest cemetery, then fixed Max with a penetrating gaze, 'you'll end up like our father. *Morte.*'

'That will not happen to me,' he said, balling his fingers into a fist. 'I am nothing like our father.'

'No, you're not. You are loyal, honest and immensely generous to the people you care about—nothing like our father. But you are an unrelenting workaholic like he was. No better than an addict, because despite all your willpower, all your determination, all your talent, all your wealth you can't stop working. My God, you even live above your office.'

'*Mia sorella,* even if I wanted to go finger painting, which I do not, there is no way I can get away. People need me. I cannot just walk away without everything collapsing.'

'Even geniuses need time out to replenish. Super-heroes too,' she laughed. 'You, Clark Kent, need a rest from being Superman, a week out of this world. Not eternity. I will take care of things until you're back.'

The blood vessel in his temple pulsed, whether out of conviction or rebellion he didn't know, but her suggestion was not without merit. His sister had proven herself capable in so many ways since her appointment to Director of Public Relations.

He leaned back in his chair, steepling his fingers against his lips as he savored a compelling idea. What if he could achieve several goals by leaving Italy? While he did not believe in fate, he did believe in destiny. Was it not destiny after all that had led him to this career, launching him from male model to CEO of a multi-billion dollar empire?

Max began to wonder if his recent conversation with some Fijian silk merchants was also pre-destined. Until that meeting he hadn't known there was such a large population of Indians in Fiji, and he'd been intrigued by the innovative textile developments they had shared with him.

And he could maximize efficiencies by going undercover and checking out his hotel chain in the Pacific. Yes, he thought, warming to the idea, perhaps a change of scene, getting away from all things European might just revive his flagging spirits.

His creativity was blocked, young designers were licking at his heels. He needed to continually innovate, but nothing inspired him. The plan was worth considering after all. Nothing else had worked. Plus it would get Sophia off his case. And the art therapy gimmick she was so convinced he needed?

What could any dowdy art therapist do to him that he couldn't control?

3

______

'First time to Fiji?' the porter asked art therapist Issy Riley as they wove past the rows of poolside loungers. Bronzed men and women wearing barely-there swimsuits tanned their lithe bodies beneath the last rays of the sun.

Issy was by far the most uniquely dressed, she thought euphemistically, gazing beyond the pool to the azure sea, fringed with coconut trees. Some, no doubt, would argue she was, in fact, the worst-dressed person at the resort, but then she'd never cared for fashion.

She pushed up the sleeves of the yellow shaggy pile of her jumper as two women sauntered past, tanned from crown chakra to pink toenails, their double d-cups jiggling like caramel panacottas.

Surrounded by an ocean of virtual nakedness Issy felt prudish dressed head-to-toenails in winter discomfort. Certainly less chic than the five-year old meandering past, resplendent in streaming caftan and matching overly bejeweled sandals, snapping the sunset with her iPhone.

'Yes. First time anywhere overseas, actually,' she ran her

fingers over the roll of her turtleneck, wishing she'd thought to wear a tee-shirt so she could peel the jumper off.

As always she'd left things too late. She'd been in a mad panic to get to the plane and hadn't even thought to pack spare clothes to change into once she'd arrived at Nadi airport.

Taking refuge beneath a palm tree Issy momentarily relaxed as a choir of Fijian men and women dressed in flowing white gowns began to sing in the open area just beyond the pool. Their voices soared through the humid air. Then suddenly realizing they were singing Christmas carols tension knotted her shoulders.

Christmas.

When she'd offered to help her business partner Nancy, and take this last minute client, she'd thought she could escape the festive season, dripping with tinsel and baubles, and the promise of happiness.

Her fingers tightened around the note the receptionist had passed her when she'd checked in. At least work meant she wouldn't have to spend the holiday season at her mother's with HIM—the traitorous, lying, three-timing control-freak of a fiancé. Make that ex-fiancé, she corrected. She had dumped him immediately, but that didn't stop her heart from taking a hit.

Issy stared into the distance her attention diverted by a huge Christmas tree blazing with a rainbow of colored lights. She closed her eyes and sighed. Why couldn't she find a promise-keeper?

Married by Christmas? Nope. Once again the bus of happily-ever-after failed to pull up at her stop, but to find out on Facebook that James was cheating on her weeks before their wedding? No one deserved that humiliation.

Even if her mother still thought James was the best thing

since sliced toast, at least Issy had the balls to shut down his lies, the courage to confront the truth, the strength to face life on her own again. She swallowed hard as the sharp edge of betrayal ran a ragged line through her chest. She'd had a lucky escape.

The porter smiled stiffly as though sensing her discomfort. 'Holiday?'

Issy looked longingly at people relaxing by the pool, her gaze hovering over a loved-up couple entwined on a sun-lounger. She felt a tug of disappointment. Would she ever trust enough to fall in love again? She crushed the note from her client in her hands, pressing her lips together as she turned away. 'Business.'

All the men in her life, even her father, had let her down terribly. Work was a most welcome distraction. She didn't need a man in her life, she reminded herself. Not anymore.

A riot of shouts from the beach pulled her attention toward a group of men jabbing at something writhing on the sand at the edge of the lagoon. Whether it was an instinctive sense of brutality etched in the men's postures or the impact of the powerful figure brushing past her, she didn't know, but every whisper of her body hair stood erect.

Issy watched mesmerized, adrenaline lapping her body as a 6 foot 3 Adonis with olive toned six-pack abs and a body that could easily grace a billboard strode toward the men on the beach, clad only in tiny trunks.

He looked strangely familiar in an unfamiliar sort of way, like a celebrity in a magazine, the same handsomeness, and aloof assurance, although she knew she'd never met him before. He looked like a movie star, only tougher? Certainly not a man anyone would forget.

His muscles rippled gold fire under the heat of the fading tropical sun as, with powerful, lithe steps like a panther about to lunge, the titan advanced upon the men on the beach. Fear shadowed their faces as they turned to each other, eyes widening, aware this was no normal man approaching but a warrior, a leader of men, a man not to be defied.

'*Allora*! Stop!' His rich honey-toned voice, edged with a deep sultry Italian accent, sent shivers coursing through her body.

Tearing her eyes away from this perfect specimen of a man Issy perched on her toes, squinting under the bright sun to see what the titan was so vigorously trying to protect.

'Sea snake. Very poisonous,' the porter said.

Danger.

The warning flashed red in her mind and jackknifed through the air. Was it the snake she was afraid of or the rush of molten emotion the stranger incited?

'Come and see,' the porter beckoned.

She hesitated, torn between fear and fascination. Her pulse hammered, pummeled by the unexpected handsomeness of the man and stricken with curiosity. What sort of person would go to a snake's rescue?

For the first time in forever she felt excited, alive, her body on edge, ablaze. Why, when she was officially off men, and as she walked toward him did every whisper of hair on her body stand alert?

She frowned, trying to remember any man ever having inflamed such a reaction, as his muscular arms took the sticks from the assailants. Arms that could crush an opponent or protect a woman against his powerful lean body.

'We're only trying to protect the resort guests from danger,' the men shouted.

'*Che cavolo*! Can you not see the baby snake?' he jabbed his finger towards the rocks. 'Would you deprive it of its mother?' His eyes were a lethal shade of gunpowder blue, his gaze unyielding, freezing the men in a chilly silence. 'She will not strike unless provoked.'

Issy's breath caught in ragged gasps as she glanced at the tiny snake lingering in the distant shadows. Was this guy for real? Someone like her, who cared nothing for the senseless killing of animals.

'We didn't see it. We didn't think,' they said, stepping back. 'Sorry, Sir.'

Issy smiled, her body flooding with something that felt uncomfortably like admiration. She dragged her eyes from him and focused on the snake lying washed ashore, exposed in its vulnerability.

As dangerous as the snake was alleged to be the artist in her was captivated by the beauty of its iridescent pearl and obsidian stripes. But she was wary too, of its potent power. Was the snake feigning death or was it spellbound, against its will, offering herself to the giant of a man before her?

Issy's heart seemed to freeze then pounded like the sea crashing on the distant reef. She could relate to feeling out of her depth. She stole a glance at the knight without armor standing in far too skimpy trunks as with soft, deft movements that belied his powerful physique, he gently nudged the snake toward the sea.

Issy kept her gaze firmly on the snake as it uncoiled slowly, writhing in the wet sand as Issy drew closer to its rescuer. She stood a body's length away from him, agonizingly aware of the rich luster of his full head of blue-black wavy hair, his impeccably shaven jaw, and the intoxicating aroma of his cologne coiling through the balmy air. Earthy, sensual, exhilarating.

What was up with that, she wondered bamboozled by the commotion clanging through her mind. Her eyes recklessly savored every contoured edge of the Adonis's body as he stood at the water's edge watching the snake slither to free-dom. She traced his broad, bronzed, well-oiled chest, before sliding down the tantalizingly playful coils of soft dark hair dividing his sculptured six pack and marching a confident line from his navel, before vanishing below the rim of his tiny 'spray on' trunks.

Suddenly the Adonis turned toward her and she was immediately captured in the web of his intense blue eyes.

Issy looked away quickly. Too quickly.

Sprung!

Her face flamed carmine red as she studied her feet, wishing the escaping waves of rose pink hair that fell over her face as she did so would hide her indefinitely. After a brief moment she glanced up, hoping he had not read her mind when she'd gawked at him. The smirk on his face and the intensity of his gaze left her in no doubt he'd registered her attraction.

'Thank you for saving the snake Mr Johnstone,' said the porter, offering him a towel as he went to his side.

'Johnstone?' her voice eked out. Her eyes ping-ponged between the stranger and the porter. Thrusting her hand in her pocket, she unfurled the note the receptionist had given her. Issy's stomach dived a nervous somersault that would have done an Olympic swimmer proud as she reread the message, studying the words forged in firm, confident handwriting—no sign of weakness anywhere. "Meet me by the pool. (Signed) Mr. Johnstone."

Oh, God. Mortification coiled through her body. 'You can't be *that* Mr. Johnstone.'

He stared at her as if she was insane.

She bit her lip, holding back any attempt at an explanation for her earlier behavior that she knew would only dig a deeper hole. 'There must be some mistake.'

DID YOU ENJOY READING THIS EXCERPT

Did you enjoy reading this excerpt?
Married by Christmas is available now in eBook and Print
from all good online bookstores.

Read on for a sneak peek into Mollie's upcoming book
Claimed by The Sheikh

EXCERPT: FLIGHT OF PASSION

FLIGHT OF PASSION

BOOK ONE IN THE TRUE LOVE SERIES AVAILABLE NOW

Past love and the obsessions that bind them.

Devastatingly handsome Oliver Hart is used to getting what he wants. Single, thirty-five and a committed bachelor, he plays by his own rules. On a personal quest to catch a rare, elusive and very valuable butterfly, he's unwittingly distracted by a former flame, Ruby Diaz—a woman who callously abandoned him eight years earlier.

Deciding he wants to reclaim the beauty as his own, in his mind, it's as good as done.

But Ruby is not his for the taking. Promised to the son of a wealthy landowner, she refuses to succumb to his charms. On a quest to save her family's land, Ruby knows she must put duty first, and silence the passionate stirrings of her heart. But Oliver doesn't make things easy for her. He's not taking no for an answer.

Risking everything to help the woman he loves to gain her freedom, Oliver entangles himself in an emotional net that alters his life forever. Sacrificing his own selfish pursuit to help Ruby, he realizes that you may be able to own something, but you can never own someone—especially the women you love.

Have you ever wanted to be with someone who sent your heart soaring but threatens your sense of security? Someone who lifts you clear out of the water, but you're not sure will be around to catch you when you fall head over heels in love? Flight of Passion is a rapturous tale of beauty, obsession and the transformational power of unconditional love.

which it is easy to lose oneself—I really felt like I had been to Mexico by the time I had finished. Her butterfly theme echoes throughout the book both literally and figuratively. The main characters, Oliver and Ruby, are each conflicted in their own ways. Despite facing challenges, both ultimately find the strength to work through their difficulties to emerge better people, and most importantly, triumph over adversity together. A touching and heart-warming book, well worth a read."

~ Cathy Rioran

"Fast paced, heart wrenching, completely unexpected twists, excellent storyline, and a hell of a good read. You just gotta love Mollie's imagination and expertise in her writing."

~ Rae Waterhouse

"I fell in love with Ruby and Oliver, they are so good for each other, but both are so filled with garbage that their families filled them with, that they can't see what's in front of them. And when they finally realize that diamonds don't have a hold to what they had, they are about to lose it. The butterflies remind me of how ethereal life is and it is up to us to not waste it, but live the fullest and best we can."

~ Advance reviewer

"I really enjoyed Flight of Passion! I loved the descriptions of the butterflies and of the setting of the farm in Mexico. Wonderfully descriptive writing that transports you to a golden orchard filled with butterflies. Perfect for a cold winter's evening curled up by the fire."

~ Linda Buckhingham

PROLOGUE

GROWING UP OLIVER WAS LEFT WITH THE impression he wasn't worthy. First by his parents who at the age of four sent him to the bottom of the world. It was as if they didn't know what to do with their infinitely curious and energetic child. It was as if sending him to the most prestigious boarding school in New Zealand absolved them of their responsibility, the responsibility which was every parents—or should be, he thought bitterly—to love their child unconditionally.

After his run in with a box of matches they told him he would amount to nothing. He proved them wrong. At sixteen he left New Zealand and headed for New York. It was true. If he could make it there he could make it anywhere. With the ruthless determination he was both admired and feared for like King Kong on steroids he quickly climbed to the top of the property acquisition tree.

He was king of the beasts, the man everyone wanted at their dreary New York parties, full of checkbook philanthropists who would never stoop to get close to the people their showy donations benefitted. Parties, like the one where he'd first met Ruby Diaz

Ruby had fluttered into his life like a breath of fresh air. She had lit up the room with her illuminating presence and dazzlingly rare beauty, not just on the outside, but the inside too. Her authenticity had the scent of violets—too guileless for pretense.

His darling Ruby. Oliver swallowed hard, refusing to succumb to the wave of angry hurt that swum from his heart to his throat.

For three blissful years they were inseparable. But no matter how much success he acquired, how extraordinarily wealthy he became, he wasn't good enough for the Diaz's darling Ruby. He never knew why she flew from his life, disappearing as quickly as she'd arrived. She had said nothing, given him no explanation, not even the courtesy of a call.

The Diaz family and the way Ruby had callously abandoned him reminded Oliver he would never be worthy—he was unlovable. Perhaps he should thank them for sparing him further hurt. Thanks to them and his hopeless parents he swore never to love again.

And that suited him just fine.

OBSESSION

I would like to be the air that inhabits you

~ Margaret Atwood ~

1

———

WOULD SELLING *BUTTERFLY LOVERS* REALLY free him of painful memories he'd rather forget?

Common sense told Oliver Hart that *Butterfly Lovers* was just a painting. An inanimate object, incapable of controlling him. But that was the trouble—it did control him, seducing him with its beauty, twisting his heart with bittersweet memories.

He'd intended to keep it . . . her . . . forever. His heartbeat seemed to almost stop as he thought of Ruby Diaz, the woman who had inspired the painting's commission. He rubbed his powerful chest, trying to ease the painful tightness that constricted his lungs as he surveyed the crowd gathered for the charity art auction.

It was time to let them both go. But would he ever be free?

His gaze swept over the minimalist, exquisitely designed interior, lingering over the priceless abstract by Rothko adorning a charcoal-black wall, at Hillcrest, his newly acquired mansion, and New Jersey's most expensive country estate.

Tonight, though, it was *Butterfly Lovers* which held in its grip women dripping with diamonds, and men clad in Armani. Locked in shared awe, they clustered around the painting, studying every line, every pulsating color.

Oliver wondered if their eyes ached as his did with a heady mix of pleasure and pain just to stand in its spellbinding presence. Or were they trying to decode the painting's hidden secrets?

Like a moth to a seductive flame, his eyes drifted to the bottom of the painting. Nobody, but one other person, would ever be able to decipher the graffiti-styled line of poetry scrawled in throbbing orange along the bottom of the painting.

Painful memories bled into his consciousness. Why the hell couldn't he shake her?

Butterfly Lovers. The painting was aptly named, he mused forcing his mind from the woman who had inspired the purchase. The dancing kaleidoscope of color reminded Oliver of his collection of exotic butterflies—his hobbyhorse and quiet obsession.

Dazzling sapphire blues, glistening watermelon pinks, pulsating canary yellows with shimmering oranges—flew from the canvas, and ricocheted off the marble floor which had been polished to a mirror-like gleam.

He had commissioned the painting in a move of uncharacteristic impulsiveness eight years earlier when he was 22 and madly in lust with Ruby. A 20 year-old exotic beauty, she'd fluttered into his life, bringing with her eternal sunshine, and air so fresh it seeped through the iron fortress he'd built around his heart.

Butterfly Lovers encapsulated the vitality, optimism and positivity she exuded. It was a rare piece which the serious art connoisseurs who gathered here this evening would die to possess. Oliver's brow furrowed, aware many were drawn here not by the desire to possess the contemporary art world's finest paintings, but insatiable voyeurs hungry to glimpse the inner world of one of America's wealthiest and most elusive bachelors.

Immensely private, he'd never opened any of his palatial homes to the public before. Not homes, *houses*, he corrected. He congratulated himself as he glanced around the clinical, museum-like surroundings. The dark walls and sophisticated lighting, spotlighting priceless works of art, created a sophisticated, yet austere, facade. If a building was truly a reflection of its owner, as many designers believed, the interior aptly reinforced the stereotypes perpetuated in the media—moody, dark, mysterious and strictly hands-off.

There was some truth to that, but it was not the whole truth.

Oliver's eyes drifted to the spiraling staircase and the heavy gold braided rope barricading the entrance to the upper level. He never let anyone get beyond the ground floor of his psyche. Some tried, but few persevered. No one, other than Ruby had ever penetrated his fortified armor. And that was a mistake.

He was complicated.

No doubt someone here tonight would go home and tweet that he was something of a social outcast, and arrogant to boot, Oliver thought as he hovered in the background. The fact was that he preferred his own company to engaging with his guests—predominantly wealthy financiers and bankers.

He knew his contempt was hypocritical, given he didn't care who reached into their pockets. But there was something decidedly unpalatable about bankers and the merciless way they preyed on the vulnerable. Tonight, he would gladly encourage them to part with their millions.

As he glanced at his reflection in the floor length window it struck him how far he had come from the days when just finding money to support himself and his little sister had been a struggle. Resplendent in an immaculately tailored Dolce & Gabbana tuxedo cut from the finest Italian wool, he looked like he belonged.

Oliver rubbed his hand over his pecs, powerfully aware of the Maori-inspired tattoo coiled over his shoulder that the crisp white linen of his shirt concealed. His hands pulsed with renewed conviction. It was his touchstone—a symbolic reminder that he was fierce and untouchable—a warrior businessman and an impenetrable lover.

On a good day, he even fooled himself.

But no matter how easy it was to make millions, no matter how many things he acquired, he'd never found a sense of contentment.

Except with—

Oliver bit down on his teeth, grinding them together in a futile attempt to crush memories he was determined not to revisit.

He glanced at his Rolex. 7:03:02. Irritability coursed through his veins. What the hell was the auctioneer waiting for? He fixed him with a piercing look, firing his unspoken annoyance through the crowd.

Tardiness was something he abhorred, and doubly-so tonight, he thought as he locked on the important call he had to make. In one hour it would be 8am in New Zealand and his sister, as punctual as he was, would be anxiously waiting.

As though feeling the pointed tip of Oliver's anger the auctioneer looked up. His relaxed smile quickly shattered as he was forced to confront the aggressive glint in Oliver's eyes, the rigid set of his shoulders, the brutally hard line of his jaw.

The auctioneer banged his hardwood gavel on the sounding block with short urgent thuds, his florid face ballooning as the chatter continued.

"Ladies and gentlemen, can I have your attention?" More insistent hammering. "Attention! Attention!"

The chatter fell to an orderly whisper, extinguished finally by the auctioneer's solemn voice.

"As you know, tonight is a unique opportunity to savor the extraordinary passions of Oliver Hart. Renowned as an astute business man, Oliver Hart is also an obsessive collector," he said.

"He has one of the most significant collations of contemporary art in the world. Not only a man of significant wealth, Oliver Hart, founder of Hart Luxury Hotel Consortium, is a man of outstanding generosity. All the funds raised by tonight's art auction will provide relief for those affected by last month's devastating earthquake in New Zealand, where he spent much of his childhood."

Oliver studied his feet as a thunder of applause quaked through the room, amplifying as it echoed off the walls.

Childhood.

The word was like a vicious punch to his stomach. Oppressive memories pounded his brain, and this time there was no silencing them.

Suddenly he was four years old again. Four years old and frightened. Lonely. Abandoned. Trapped in a jungle of strangers. Abandoned by bickering parents into a boarding school, neither one willing to let the other have custody. Selfishly caring more about winning against each other than the needs of their own child. And then there was his father.

His jaw locked as he bit down hard, swallowing a toxic

cocktail of grief and anger. The brutal beatings hadn't hurt nearly as much as the verbal abuse and discouragement he'd suffered when he told them he wanted to be like his grandfather and study butterflies. The abuse had only intensified when he turned his back on the legal career his father had wanted. *'You'll never achieve anything. I wish you'd never been born. How dare you defy me you worthless piece of shit,'* the pain of these beatings had long healed—but those words still hurt.

Freezing sweat clung to Oliver's body in a vice-like grip, as he recalled the scorn his father rained upon him during his few personal visits. He paced across to the open window, inhaling deeply as he struggled to rip himself free from the shards of the past. Jesus, what sort of father tries to have his son institutionalized?

To some, it might seem ironic that he should be so generous to a country where he spent such an unhappy childhood, but Oliver didn't like to think of others suffering.

He forced his mind back to the present.

"Tonight's opening painting *Butterfly Lovers* is a significant artwork," the auctioneer continued, glancing down at his notes.

Oliver didn't have to read his words to know that what he would reveal was a shallow rendition of the truth. Only two people in the world truly knew just what *Butterfly Lovers* meant.

He glanced around the room thinking Ruby might have come, hoping with all his willpower she hadn't.

2

H E FORCED HIMSELF NOT TO BETRAY THE turmoil of emotions jack-knifing through his body as the massive painting was carried to the makeshift podium.

The butterfly theme had held so much promise. He'd never really bought into Ruby's tales about the transformative power of art to heal. But back then privately he'd hoped her optimism might rub off. With her by his side, and by owning the painting, perhaps he could shed a skin, free himself of his deformed past, re-emerge in a new skin. Undamaged. Someone nearing perfection. A better man. The sort of man Ruby deserved.

He'd been a fool.

Oliver's spine stiffened. He'd intended to keep it . . .

her . . . forever. But even good intentions couldn't make up for a lifetime's inability to commit. He moved towards the terrace, widening the distance between him and the painting. He would no longer succumb to the painting's potent power to remind him of his failings.

"Created specifically for Oliver over seven years ago by

struggling contemporary artist CG Tombly—only Oliver could have foreseen its financial potential."

Oliver's brow furrowed. The suggestion he had acquired the painting for commercial gain, rankled him. If he wasn't such a private man he might have told the crowd the truth. He'd made the mistake of talking candidly once before—a mistake he wouldn't be making again.

In its place he'd created a new habit—a habit of keeping his emotional life to himself, one he wasn't about to break. Soon the painting, and the painful memories of the only woman capable of making him feel, would be shed and he could devote himself to less painful obsessions.

"As always, Oliver's timing is impeccable. The painting's value has rocketed in the same soaring capacity as the palatial hotel Oliver's company has recently constructed in Dubai–so high it almost touches the gods."

The auctioneer flung his hands into the air to accentuate his point. "Oliver Hart," he said, nodding in his direction and pointing to his towering 6-foot, 2-inch frame, "never does anything small."

Oliver thrust his hands in his pockets and glanced out the window refusing to look at the painting as the bidding began.

In a few fist-clenching minutes it would all be over and he could get on with his life.

His gaze drifted to the sculpture garden, lying beyond the pool, alighting on a solitary bronze sculpture by Brancusi. The modernist interpretation of Hercules holding the world on his shoulders, with its roughly hewn egg shaped sphere symbolizing earth had always appealed to him.

Balanced precariously on a towering sculpted wood base, the odd shape and the large crater severing the middle of the sphere challenged conventional notions of perfection and reminded him of humanity's rawness.

As his gaze lingered over the sculpture it occurred to him that repairing his scars, so deep that no relationship he started ever endured, required a Herculean effort.

No wonder the painting had failed.

But he still wanted to believe, as the ancient Greeks had, that art had a powerful ability to transform lives. He only hoped that selling the painting finally fulfilled this purpose. Perhaps then the painful memories that still haunted him could be turned to good.

He turned and fixed his gaze upon the audience. Who would be its new owner he wondered as the opening bid of one million was made. Would it go to Don Hermes, the impotent pharmaceutical giant, standing just ahead of him, or some other equally innocuous purchaser? Or would some anonymous bidder calling from China, Europe or the Middle East be the lucky buyer?

"$12 million? Do I have $12 million?" The bags under the auctioneer's eyes shifted as he tilted his head forward, and peered under his glasses.

"A small price to pay," he continued, his gaze briefly flickering to Oliver, "for a painting personally commissioned by a man who defies every category and transcends every cliché: a man with tremendous gusto and creative generosity."

The auctioneer's eyes flew to a scantily dressed blonde hovering hopefully next to Oliver. "A man who has yet to be pinned down."

Oliver caste her a dismissive look and moved further toward the back of the room.

"$12 million we have," cried the auctioneer's assistant, nodding vigorously as he pressed his iPhone firmly to his ear.

Oliver's heart lurched as the bidding began.

"$13 million," the assistant taking telephone bids shouted, raising his hand.

"$13.2 million." The auctioneer's eyes darted between the phone bidder and two men determined to claim the painting as their own.

Explosive tension hovered as one of the two remaining bidders turned their attention away.

"$13.5 million! At $13.5 million the painting will be sold," the auctioneer warned. He suspended the gavel in the air, pausing as he scanned the room.

"$17.4 million," came a guttural, low growl from the front of the crowd.

A record price!

The room fell silent under the weight of the bid, then buzzed with irritatingly discordant voices, their murmurs of awe and envy a rising tide of white noise.

Oliver's eyes darted to the front row. Over $14 million? The price was ridiculous. Someone must want it desperately. But who and why?

He was acquainted with the deep pockets of unbridled obsession. He understood intimately the seductive power of the painting.

But this was crazy bidding.

There had to be a compelling reason surpassing the usual appreciation of an art-lover. At that price it could hardly be an investment buy.

So that left . . . what?

Oliver paced the back of the room in agitation unable to see the face of the man who had placed this latest bid. He caught a glimpse of the woman next to the anonymous bidder as she shook a sexy spill of sun-kissed curls down her back. The familiar gesture sent shockwaves to his heart.

It couldn't be.

Her head turned slightly.

Oliver stood still, as if immobile, as if turned to stone.

Ruby Diaz.

His Ruby.

3

A SYMPHONY OF EMOTIONS CRASHED through his veins as he saw a possessive arm snake around Ruby's waist and realized with horror the identity of the serpent she was with. Oliver threw back his shoulders, his muscular jaw tilted forward in defiance as he looked at the nauseatingly familiar figure.

Carlos Torres, the New York based, Mexican banking magnate and the-soon-to-be owner of *Butterfly Lovers.*

He could not let his painting—their painting—fall into her lover's clutches—a man as unscrupulous as he was deceptively charming.

Oliver's overactive mind raced with scenarios. He could draw from his own accounts the money for the earthquake fund—adding to the millions he had already donated.

But he knew with chilling certainty he was powerless to flout protocol, to bend the rules, to manipulate the outcome to suit his own desires. He knew only too well that once the auction had started, *Butterfly Lovers* could not be withdrawn.

"At this price, we'll sell," the auctioneer's eyes swept the room for any last bids.

The muscles in Oliver's chest tightened as he saw the auctioneer's gavel ascend into the air.

He watched helplessly as Carlos pulled Ruby toward him and folded her into his arms. The bitter taste of jealousy flooded his mouth.

The gavel sank toward the sounding block with freeze-frame inevitability. A splintering crack as wood met wood confirmed it was over with chilling clarity.

Oliver's hand tightened into a closed fist, crumpling the *Butterfly Lovers* catalogue into obscurity.

His heart rate pulsated making his chest feel as though it was about to implode, as Ruby turned and he watched with shock the way she wilted under Carlos' dominant presence, the light of passion missing from her eyes. She seemed sad and vulnerable—and the Ruby he knew was neither.

Something was wrong.

His rational mind thundered a warning. Don't get involved.

What business was it of his if she wanted to make a life with that snake? None. Not ordinarily. But Ruby wasn't ordinary. Accepting and accommodating maybe, but something told him there was more to their union than met the eye.

He clenched his fists and cursed softly fighting against the impulse to save her from a big mistake. Playing rescuer would invite complications he didn't need.

Especially now.

What he needed was a distraction. What he needed was uncomplicated sex—not to reignite an obsession. Ruby had already proven herself capable of breaking his heart mercilessly.

Not so with paintings and sculptures and his beloved butterflies, he mused, forcing his thoughts back to his collections. Once possessed they would never leave without his consent. And he could never make them cry. His jaw clenched as bitter memories of his parents' feuding pounded in his ears. His mother's heart-wrenching cries once heard, never forgotten.

He must not be distracted. He must not allow Ruby to get close. Obviously she had engineered Carlos to buy the painting, knowing full well how it would torture Oliver. She tortured him all those years ago and it was clear she intended to continue the onslaught. She could have that damned painting, he mused as unwelcome, undesired, uncontrollable passions, long forgotten but now unbridled, threatened to escape.

He rested one shoulder against the floor length window, his attention locked on Ruby as she freed herself from Carlos' clutches and fluttered through the swelling crowd toward the patio.

She possessed an innate and natural elegance that caused his glands to salivate, wetting his appetite in open defiance of his will. Her legs screamed danger—their long, slender length accented in scorchingly sharp stilettos that threatened to kill.

Kill his resolve. Kill his self-control. Kill him all over again.

He reached for a glass of whiskey from a passing waitress. He rocked the glass from side to side and studied the rough ice-chunks crashing through the amber liquid, then knocked the drink back, drowning his conflicting emotions.

Like a moth drawn to light he savored the way her floor length, silk dress clung to her lithe figure, her hibiscus red dress shimmering under the halogen lights like the wings of a newly emerged butterfly.

The way the vibrant color of her dress contrasted so deliciously with the flock of black cocktail dresses and designer dark suits everyone else favored brought a smile to his lips. Ruby had always stood out from the crowd.

Walk away, stay away. The voice in his head pitched high and shrill like an ambulance siren, as he fought an instinctive need to free her from a bad mistake.

The irregularly cut crystal pressed into his fingers as he gripped the glass. His life had rapidly become complicated.

He craned his neck as he momentarily lost sight of her, searching over the sea of heads and glittering diamonds.

Like the shards of ice in his glass, his hardened intention to stay detached was fracturing.

Plastering on a face of extreme nonchalance, he pushed determinedly towards her through the crowd as she stepped onto the patio and gazed forlornly up at the stars.

Why the hell was she with a dickhead like Carlos.

Glancing at his watch, Oliver wondered if he could find out what he needed to know in less than 20 minutes?

DID YOU ENJOY READING THIS EXCERPT?. . .

Thank you for purchasing and reading my books. You are more than my livelihood—you let me live my passion. Without your love of romance and belief in the power of love, this book would never have been born. I really hope you loved this excerpt from my full-length novel *Flight of Passion* as much as I enjoyed writing it.

Purchase the full-length copy and discover what happens next.

Flight of Passion: Book One in the True Love series available now from all good bookstores

Flight of Passion: Book One in the True Love series available now from all good bookstores

Here's to an extra-ordinary level of love and happiness in all our lives.

With love,

that the child isn't their biological son. Salim is Tariq's son, with his former lover, a renowned architect.

Three years ago, after being banished by Tariq from his desert kingdom, Melanie Jones secretly gave her baby to Tariq's childless brother and his wife, in a swap the world was never supposed to know about.

The tragedy pulls her back to the world that rejected her and the man who abandoned her--the only man capable of turning her carefully controlled world upside down.

Tariq will do whatever it takes to protect his legacy, including claiming Melanie as his bride and his son as heir before scandals ensue.

But Melanie has other plans for her future—a westernized life where she's free to operate her own business and control her own life.

If you love true romance and beautiful love stories, set against a sensuous backdrop of the desert, art, and architecture you'll love *Claimed by The Sheikh.*

Book two in the *True Love* series available now, in audio, paperback and eBook

Claimed
By The Sheikh
MOLLIE
MATHEWS

CLAIMED BY THE SHEIKH

THE SHEIKHS UNTAMED BRIDES

MOLLIE MATHEWS

CLAIMED BY THE SHEIKH

BOOK TWO IN THE TRUE LOVE SERIES.

Available now

A grief-stricken Sheikh Tariq na Hassir, the formidable ruler of the Kingdom of Avana, arrives in Paris to claim his brother's child after a car crash killed his parents--only to find out from the hospital that the child isn't their biological son. It's Tariq's son, with his former lover.

Three years ago, after being banished by Tariq from his desert kingdom, renown architect Melanie Jones secretly gave her baby to Tariq's childless brother and his wife, in a swap the world was never supposed to discover.

The tragedy pulls her back to the world that rejected her and the man who abandoned her—the only man capable of tuning her carefully controlled world upside down.

Tariq will do whatever it takes to protect his legacy, including claiming Melanie as his bride and his son as heir before scandals ensue. But Melanie has other plans for her future—a westernized life where she's free to operate her own business and control her own life.

Join Mollie's new release newsletter here http://eepurl.com/cigEsH. Be the first to know when *the next book in the series* is released.

Dear Friends,

I hope you enjoy *Claimed by the Sheikh*. It touches on a number of subjects I love and care about with the twists and turns in the plot. I always love celebrating the strength of the human spirit, and what people do when faced with seemingly insurmountable challenges in their lives, and how unexpected events can turn disaster or tragedy into something good.

I love the fact that Melanie follows an unusual path as a pioneering architect. I love how hard she works at it. I always enjoy exploring how each of us uses and expresses our particular talents. And I felt a bond with her, because I too studied architecture—but I didn't have the courage and determination that Melanie had to finish.

Watching Melanie struggle with discrimination, knockbacks, and success, and the price you pay for them, was familiar to me too. Each person lives success differently and her adventures along the way help her become the person she is destined to be. Whatever your path in life, you have a gift. Something nobody else can do as beautifully and skillfully as you.

How you express it, how you live it, and how you share it with others is unique to you. You have your own special way of dealing with life and the talents you've been given, whether you hide those gifts or share them openly.

I hope you enjoy reading about this talented young architect, and following her story as it unfolds. Victory and success come in many forms and guises, her path is an exciting, fascinating, and re- warding one, and I'm sure yours will be too!

With all my love,
Mollie

PRAISE FOR CLAIMED BY THE SHEIKH

"Wow, just wow, I can't articulate enough how compellingly page-turning this remarkable story was. If I could give it more than 5 stars this would be it! This author has the gift & the power to make you experience her remarkable craft on a whole other level. I was drawn into the story when she shared a few chapters with me quite a while ago now & I'm beyond thrilled that she managed to finish it. I'm not one to tell the story, the blurb & other reviewers will cover that but I will concede that this magical, mystical, hauntingly beautiful story will stay with me for the longest time. Highly recommended."

~ **Terry Babb**

"Claimed by the Sheikh was a fast paced read that held my interest from the first page to the last. The story had a depth to the characters and strong imagery due to the author's attention to details. Watching two worlds collide, as well as two strong characters fight for what they each believe is right, just added another layer to the story.

I enjoy books that are set in the desert with desert royalty or sheikhs. Claimed by the Sheikh was a strong story with a depth to the characters of both Tariq and Melanie who we get to know a little at a time as well as their history from three years before. They seem to have unresolved issues and feelings for each other but given their differences will it be any different this time around? There was very strong imagery due to the vivid descriptions of the scenery, the palace and Melanie's drawings, which made me feel that I was there. Tariq's rescue of endangered animals and his philanthropy was a nice addition to the story. I liked how the child, Salim, was brought into the story as well as his importance to the story line. Ms. Mathews is fast becoming a favorite author."

~ JoAnne

"This book grabbed me from the first page. Both lead characters were portrayed fully as real people not just by how they looked as in many books. There being a child involved added to my enjoyment!"

~ Melba

"The tone for this book is set in the opening chapters as the young Sheikh is faced with ongoing difficulties in the kingdom created by his atrocious father. He is fighting an ongoing battle to prevent himself from being sucked into the past and to rather create a new and prosperous future for his people. Tariq's previous rejection of Melanie and the results have soured her against romantic love and made her determined to carve a career for herself."

~ Margaret

"I really like the premise of the book, I always like the royal romance with impediments to happiness and this book has it in spades. I like the strong figure of the Sheikh and the strong heroine who has built a professional career. Immediately I can see lots of problems that seem insurmountable at first: their past stormy relationship, the baby secret, her desire to have her own career, his desire for an heir, his demand to raise the child, his vow to swear off women. I also like that, right of the bat, we learn about his plan to build a reserve for animals and to right the many wrongs from his father's legacy. These are all good foundations for a fiery, passionate and conflicting relationship."

~ Elaine

"Fantastic premise that has a substantial conflict behind it. I like Melanie a lot. A strong female heroine is what I want to read. I think that is particularly important with such a powerful man, and here in this instance, someone who can wield such power. I love love love the beginning. This is one tough guy but the book opens with him protecting a baby giraffe. Fantastic opening."

~Leanne

"Tariq's emotional conflict is that he is in love with Melanie and won't admit it to himself. As a reader, it keeps me on pins and needles to see if Tariq realizes it himself."

~ Tonni

"It hooked me, it was impactful and well written. Sexual

tension is always a plus for me and I loved the strong characters."

~ Terry

"I wanted to keep reading. It was intriguing."

~Robyn

"Claimed by the Sheikh has an intriguing plot: keeping the Sheikh's illegitimate child a secret through all the complications that arise. The main characters, Melanie as the independent architect and Tariq as the wealthy, powerful Sheikh of a fictitious Arab country are well fleshed out and believable. You have empathy for their situation and the tension about whether the secrets will be revealed carries you through the book. This is the stuff of fairy tales. The book does go a long way towards helping the reader understand Tariq's Islamic beliefs and his commitment to helping his people and the endangered animals he wants to rescue. There is a nice subplot about Melanie's struggle to become recognized as a creative architect in a field dominated by men. Tariq's wealth comes in handy there. A good heartfelt romance."

~Elaine

PROLOGUE

The traffic on the motorway started to speed up as they got closer to Charlotte's husband's new office in the French headquarters of the Fédération Internationale de Football Association in southern France.

Salim was still asleep in the backseat when Charlie looked at her watch and realized it was nearly 1 am and they were going to be late to pick up Zayed. If he was exhausted, as he often was at the end of a long day, she knew he wouldn't wait. He had been working so hard rebuilding his life to provide for her and Salim. Tonight had been a special celebration. She was proud that he had won the election to be the new FIFA president. His campaign focused on change, football ideals and uniting warring countries through their common passion for sport. She didn't want to be late.

Charlie grabbed her iPhone from the dashboard and placed it in her lap, to send him a text, when Salim suddenly woke.

"Don't drive and text, Mommy!" he said, disapprovingly. "You'll cause an accident."

"I just want to tell Daddy that we're running a few minutes late, but we're almost there. Otherwise, he'll grab a ride with one of his staff and leave before we arrive." Charlie looked down and started texting quickly, holding the steering wheel firm with one hand.

Ten minutes later Salim saw his father first as they approached the building where he worked. "Daddy!"

Charlie pulled to the curb, got out of the car and opened the passenger door. Salim had already unbuckled his seatbelt and climbed out of his booster seat. He ran to his father.

Zayed scooped him into his powerful arms and drew Charlie to his side. His sheer strength and physicality always made her swoon and she leaned into his chest.

"*Marhabaan, habibti.* Hello, my love. How's my favorite team?" he said, placing a kiss on Charlie's lips before turning to Salim and kissing his chubby cheeks.

"You must be tired," Charlie said.

Zayed heaved a deep breath, sucking the early morning air into his lungs. "Exhausted!"

"I'll drive," Charlie said. "Why don't you sit in the back and take a nap? I don't want you to be too tired to give me some special attention when we get home," she laughed, planting a sloppy kiss on his sexy lips.

She was thinking about Melanie and how grateful she was to her sister as she embraced Salim and Zayed. She wanted to take a selfie of them and send her a text but they agreed not to stay in contact. Those were the rules. Besides they had their own busy lives in separate worlds. She wasn't obliged to call, but she wanted to. But she didn't want to upset her or retraumatize her sister either. It wouldn't be fair to her. Not when Charlie was so happy, and Melanie was all alone. *Without Salim.*

Charlie swallowed back the little trace of guilt that she never managed to kick and smiled as she watched Zayed clamber into the car, curling his long-powerful frame like a contortionist, into the back. He waited for Salim to climb in and rested his head against the booster seat and fell asleep.

She was so happy. She didn't need to be a princess. She didn't need Zayed's royal title. All she needed was her two favorite men, she thought as she pressed the keyless start and pulled out from the curb.

Charlie wanted to get home quickly. Both her boys needed to be in their beds. She hadn't wanted to leave Salim with a babysitter and was feeling a little reprehensible for lifting him from his warm bed to pick up his dad, but she knew how much Zayed had missed them both. He had been working so hard and tonight had been a well-earned celebration. Thankfully their home was only a fast 40 minute trip on the A7 autoroutes du Soleil.

They hadn't traveled far when Salim's eyes suddenly fluttered open. "You're not wearing your seatbelt!" he censured.

Charlie glanced at him in the rear-view mirror and noticed that Salim and Zayed weren't buckled in either. She'd heard the chime but had been distracted, worrying about Melanie, and how she must be suffering. She'd been rushed and stressed all day.

"Neither are you," Charlie said, turning around.

"I forgot, mommy," Salim said, he rubbed his sleepy eyes and started to put his seatbelt on, but it was caught in the door and he couldn't. He tugged and pulled on it. "It's stuck, mommy."

Charlie's heart raced as she turned to keep her eyes on the road. She was sitting right on the legal speed limit of 80 mph. It always felt so fast. Behind and in front of her was a line of other cars and there was no room to pull over. She couldn't stop now, without causing an accident.

"We'll be home in a minute, darling," she said, glancing at Salim again in the rear view mirror. The words had barely left her mouth when his eyes flew wide in horror. He saw a huge tourist bus careering toward them from the left.

PROLOGUE (CONT.)

S alim screamed. Charlie turned too late. The bus hit them with monstrous force.

Zayed woke and hurled his body across his son instinctively.

There was the sound of crushing metal and splintering glass as Charlie's cellphone flew from her hand. Salim watched in horror as his mother shot through the windshield like a torpedo. She careered through the air, and disappeared under the cars in front. Their SUV struck another, stopped abruptly, and Salim and his father were crushed amongst a mangled heap of other cars.

The bus had shunted them three lanes over. The driver lay motionless with his head on the steering wheel as people rushed from their cars toward him, and several others ran toward Charlie's car.

The sky was ablaze with tiny lights from their cellphones as people were calling the emergency services. A crowd were staring at Charlie under the vehicle where she had landed, covered with blood and broken glass. Traffic was backed up behind them, and within minutes sirens screamed in the distance. People wandered dazed and numb with shock as they surveyed the carnage.

The driver of the bus was concussed and staggered from the wreck, but there was no sign of life under the car where Charlie had landed. Salim lay beneath his father's powerful body, his head, face, and arms covered with blood. No one dared touch Salim or Zayed for fear of injuring them further. No one knew if they were alive. As they waited for the emergency services to arrive it looked hopeless. But there was so much blood and twisted metal everywhere, no one could see clearly.

A paramedic team arrived by helicopter. The crew pulled Salim and Zayed from the wreckage.

Zayed was pronounced dead and Salim was immediately assessed as in a critical condition. They inserted a breathing tube before they left the scene and airlifted him to a hospital in Montpellier with life-threatening head injuries. More paramedics and emergency services arrived, including an ambulance, sirens shrieking and lights flashing,

They removed Charlie and Zayed's body from the scene. It was hours before traffic began, moving again. In total, two people were dead, and eight people had been injured but none severely except Salim. The police and paramedics had said Zayed had died instantly when his skull was crushed against the hard surface of the television in the backseat of the car. When Charlie was thrown through the windshield and hit the pavement, she had died on impact. It was a tragedy made less horrific by knowing death had come instantly and they hadn't suffered.

The police found a blue backpack with an image of Simba from the movie The Lion King, and a soft toy of Simba too, on the floor of the car. The backpack had a name badge with Salim's name on it, and Charlie's purse with her driver's license was crushed in the front passenger seat, together with her cellphone. The screen was shattered but they could still see the picture of Charlie, Zayed, and Salim smiling on the home-screen.

Charlie and Zayed were taken to the morgue by the police. There was nothing in Charlie's purse or Zayed's wallet listing next of kin or who to notify in an accident. All they knew, for now, were their names and that they weren't French.

The paramedics had assessed that Salim had a serious head injury, a broken arm, and probably internal injuries. The police noted that none of them had been wearing seatbelts. All the police could deduce was that Charlie hadn't seen the oncoming bus, and possibly had been on her cellphone or texting. Both were common causes of accidents and fatalities. Beyond that, they knew nothing not even whether Salim would survive the accident. It looked unlikely when they'd left the scene and flew at full speed to Montpellier Hospital.

1

"Are you trying to kill her?" Tariq na Hassir, the formidable ruler of the Kingdom of Avana, seized the animal handler's arm, forcing him to release the rope laced around the baby giraffe's neck.

"She has suffered enough trauma." Tariq dismissed the man with a fierce scowl that stuck fear into enemies.

A slither of panic crept into the young man's hushed apology. "I am sorry your Excellency."

"Release the others from their cages," Tariq growled.

The man did not have to be asked twice. He knew from experience that the Sheikh's retribution for disobedience would be swift and merciless.

"You are safe from harm," Tariq said softly, stroking the baby giraffe's long neck with a gentleness that belied his strength.

"No one will ever hurt you again, Noor," he said softly, impulsively naming her as his fingertips swept through the calf 's fur. He let his long supple fingers linger a moment upon her tail. Thankfully they had saved her in time, he thought as he reached for the reins, clenching his powerful hands around the soft leather.

The rage he had first felt on hearing about the ruthless murder of the new born's mother still roared through him. Had she been executed to pay a tail dowry to the father of some money-mongering bride, he wondered? Or did some heinous person pay thousands of dollars for a wretched fly swatter?

Noor looked up and met Tariq's dark gaze. In her innocent eyes, he saw her despair, her disillusionment, her disgust with humanity. He recognized her trauma as though it was his own. Because it was.

"Humans," he said, his voice marinated with contempt. "The people you should be able to trust, the people who say they care, the people whose actions should be driven by love —the majority are driven by nothing but selfishness, deception, and lies."

Taking a bottle of milk, he placed the teat to Noor's lips. The calf 's silky black lashes grazed her cheeks as she gazed down at the foreign object then looked back at Tariq. She stared silently up at him, her eyes moist and bewildered.

Tariq had trained himself to shut down his emotions but that skill suddenly failed him. His chest trembled with suppressed rage knowing the orphaned baby would never again taste her mother's milk.

"What passes for love among some people is abhorrent," he said in a low, strained voice. "On behalf of humanity, I apologize."

The killing of the calf 's mother and three other rare Kordofan giraffes by trophy hunters seeking their tails further motivated the Sheikh's commitment to transform his anger into action.

"Do you really think you can save her?"

Tariq looked at Anwar, his younger brother by 11 months. His head was slightly bowed but he could see his eyes were fixed in sadness and longing.

Tension ripped down Tariq's spine. "Our father's reign of terror and tyranny have robbed Avana of prosperity and peace. I will make it my personal mission to right the injustices of the past. War and hostility must end. And it starts with how we treat those most vulnerable."

His fingers shook as he gripped the bottle of milk as Noor, at last, began to suckle.

An eerie silence swept across the precipitous landscape of Avana's Tiwa oasis. Tariq lifted his gaze to the horizon. The only movement visible to his naked eye was the wind etching a delicate furrow as it crawled over the golden dunes.

"Not only will I provide a sanctuary for hunted wildlife and orphans like Noor, but I will liberate God's most precious creatures from the many closing zoos and other inhumane habitats around the world," he glanced over at the other animals being unloaded from the custom-built crates.

"I will create a world-acclaimed sanctuary, impenetrable by those with impure and malicious hearts. It will be the most magical, marvelous, mesmerizingly unique place, the number one eco-tourism destination in the world. I will create meaningful employment for our people, restoring their dignity, attracting millions of visitors annually and contributing billions to the economy. But more importantly, I will show the world how kindness and compassion can be turned into plutonium and change the world."

Anwar glanced at the now lush landscape and recalled how barren it had once been. With no sign of life in sight, others had found it impossible to fathom his brother's vision to transform the punishing and unforgiving conditions into a haven for so many endangered species. Yet, as with everything Tariq turned his formidable will and mind-blowing wealth to, he had succeeded where mere mortals were destined to fail.

Anwar's heart swelled with pride as he thought of all his brother's achievements. "It's an audacious and admirable plan. And if anyone can pull it off it's you, brother. Your passion, your drive, your unrelenting ambition and pursuit of goals exceeds mere mortals. And you have the endurance and power of 13,000 Arabian horses, but aren't you setting yourself up for too much hard work? Why don't you relax? Kick back. Enjoy the fruits of your reign?" Anwar said, tossing his head in the direction of the harem. "Other men would."

"Women were our father's weakness," bitterness bled from his words. "I too once made the same mistake. I too paid the price."

There was a tense silence while Tariq lifted his gaze to the sky and studied the giant falcon circling above.

"Was it not you who once taught that your greatest weakness can also be your greatest strength?" Anwar asked.

Tariq shook his head, biting down a terse retort. "I was misled." He said, nodding his command to the animal handler lingering at a respectful distance.

He petted Noor as she was led away. "All kinds of atrocities are committed in the name of love, which is why it is the most dangerous of emotions, and why I am forever turned off to women."

2

Shielding his eyes from the blazing sun, Tariq looked skyward, honing in on the falcon's intense, focused gaze. The power, the force, the courage and the vision of the hunting dog of the sky inspired him. And unlike humans falcons were loyal—a quality Tariq valued above all else.

"The best time for a man is the time he spends with his family," he said, glancing toward his brother. "My people are my family. My animals are my family. You are my family," he said, patting his brother's shoulders.

"The first responsibility of a leader is to make his people happy and then to provide them with the required security, stability, comfort, progress and development to ensure their survival. My loyalty is to you all."

Tariq's head jerked backward sharply as he recalled the brutal tyranny of his father. "Besides what sort of man doesn't want to care for his family? Only an ego-driven tyrant like our father would turn a blind eye to the plight of our people and the cruelty imposed on God's creatures."

Tariq gritted his teeth, his jaw locking against the strain of suppressing his emotions. There was no point voicing the hostility he felt toward his father. There was no purpose in reminding his brother that his father was a behemoth, a beast, a toxic mix of oppressiveness and evilness who had wielded monstrous power and made their lives a misery.

"This has to be the most isolated place in the world," Anwar muttered, gazing out forlornly at the neutrals and as-far-as-the-eye-can-see block tones of the desert. "No wonder mother fled to London."

While Tariq missed his mother deeply he didn't share his brother's despair. He was a thirty-six-year-old ruler who was pouring his power, his infinite wealth, his heart and soul into the land and the animals who he now offered sanctuary. He was a king filled with purpose.

"There is a lot of anti-Islamic sentiment in the world. People believe we are a nation of murderers. Thanks to people who corrupt our ways for their evil agenda. Thanks to our father and his violent, corrupt rule. Thanks to warlords and governments who seek to profit from war and spread their lies. Because of all these things the international community fears us. They have been driven away. I want to bring people back here. I want to restore our nation's pride. I want to show the world the beauty and kindness of true Islam. Our people have suffered enough shaming and violence."

"Again, you have set yourself a formidable task. Are you sure you're not throwing yourself into this audacious cause just to forget about your disobedient wife?"

"My ex-wife," he corrected. His brief marriage had been a disaster. He should have resisted the arrangement. He should have refused to cement his father's power-base by marrying the daughter of his pugnacious uncle.

Loyalty. That was Tariq's weakness. Loyalty, to family, no matter the personal cost.

The marriage was as archaic as it was disastrous. But that

didn't stop Tariq wanting a family—one that didn't place demands on him he wasn't equipped to keep.

Duty—that's what counted.

The irony didn't escape him. Duty had claimed his marriage. He knew Fatima took other lovers, just like he knew that some people weren't suited to marriage. But he also knew that if he hadn't been more married to his people and his quest than he'd ever been to his wife, he might have prevented her from escaping in the night with his bodyguard in a run-down-old jeep. He might have prevented her from being buried in the sandstorm that led to her death.

He gazed out at the stark, undulating desert landscape. If he had to atone for his sins, he'd rather do it out here where there was nothing but the eerie silence and the hot wind surfing over the dunes. Where there was nothing other than his rescued wildlife meandering over what felt like the plains of the Serengeti. Where there was nothing but the blazing desert, the sand beneath his toes, and the endless Arabian sea cutting them off from the world.

Duty required sacrifice.

Tension knotted his gut as his mind drifted to the woman who angered him most. *Melanie Jones.* It had been her fault his older brother, Zayed had abdicated, and Tariq had been catapulted into the role of ruler.

Tariq vowed long ago that while he loved his older brother dearly, his disloyalty had cost too high a price. He had vowed, no matter how painful, he would never speak or think of them again.

Tariq ran his fingers down the dark brown back feathers of the hawk. "He who wants to advance should always look ahead," he said, turning to his younger brother.

"There are worse things than an eternity spent in this

beautiful kingdom of islands, miles away from anything, draped in wind and quiet, sandstorms and hot desert breezes. Anchored between the majestic desert and surrounded by the shimmering Arabian sea. You will understand the preciousness of this gift soon enough, Anwar."

The Kingdom of Avana had been the crown in the jewel of Tariq's ancestors since time began. Only this time, under his rule, instead of bloody and catastrophic wars provoked by his father's oppressive regime the Kingdom of Avana would enjoy a reign of prosperous peace.

And he'd dedicate himself to his cause—and none other. Because when he looked around Tariq didn't see the life-sentence his younger brother Anwar imagined or the chokehold his older brother Zayed felt.

He saw his home.

Yet, while he wasn't given to despair he could see his future as well as anyone if he continued alone. Today's reclusive hermit is tomorrow's bitter, old relic, he told himself, as the falcon left his arm and flew toward the object of his ardent desire.

As he watched as the giant bird of prey courted a female falcon with acrobatic displays of daring aerial feats, he was acutely aware that a kingdom wasn't a kingdom with only a king to rule. To avoid Avana falling into the clutches of his father's tyrannical offspring he needed an heir.

The possibility was as outrageous as it was urgent. To bear an heir he needed a wife. The whole idea was impossible. Once betrayed, a thousand times wiser, he reminded himself.

His dark brows curved into a frown as he saw his bodyguards gallop on horseback away from the towering walls of the palace toward him.

His body tensed with the stillness of a wild animal whose every sense was alert, suspicious and wary as they approached.

"Your Excellency! Come quickly. There's been an accident."

3

"Please, please, please choose me," Melanie Jones prayed inwardly. She swallowed hard, an ache building in her chest, as she checked her watch, then checked again as she paced the floor outside the Council administrative offices in central London. She heaved a deep breath as her thoughts raced.

Six minutes until her fate would be decided. She checked her watch again. Five minutes, 59 seconds until the officials from The Council and the other key teams assessing her architectural design for the new community library would decide her fate.

Had she done a good enough job to convince them to sign off her concept for the project? The newly elected bureaucrats in the state government had challenged her design and costings, and the whole concept was in danger of coming to a crashing end.

Had she conceded too much when she yielded to their demands to rein in her vision?

Just for once she wished she could shrug off the stigma

that dogged her when time after time, despite her award-winning designs, none of her buildings were ever constructed.

Just once she wished the vision she saw, the beauty she visualized, the joy she knew would be felt by those who eventually inhabited her buildings, was shared by those with access to the vault of money needed to bring her designs into reality.

If she could just get the dammed bureaucrats to say 'yes'. Until then she'd be nothing but a paper architect. Her life's work nothing but drawings and dreams.

Dreams.

Melanie rubbed her temple, erasing the one dream she had promised herself to forsake. *She was not going to think of him.*

Her ebony-black brows knitted in a fierce line as she forced her mind to the task at hand. She glanced down at the scatter of sketches splayed across the boardroom desk, feeling a mix of awe and pride—and aloneness.

Despite the fact that her design was breath stompingly beautiful, and searingly exquisite, her concept was also daringly innovative. The sweeping feminine curves confronted many people's sense of what architecture was and what it wasn't.

While she did everything in her power to minimize her own feminineness, in her designs aggressive masculine lines, straight edges and harsh corners were resolutely banished.

Dispelled were the sharp, angular lines and boxy shapes that so many in her field admired for their cost efficiencies. Eradicated were the shapes and forms that looked more like watchtowers in the worst of the concentration camps. Welcomed were the soaring sweeps and sensuous curves that inspired and nurtured and united people regardless of race, gender, or belief.

Melanie slid her palms over the stiff folds of her shapeless noir-black upside-down jacket. The touch of tarpaulin did an adequate job of disguising her generous breasts, but even this wouldn't detract from what many considered to be her biggest failing.

She was a woman. A woman competing in a man's world.

People, she knew only too painfully, didn't like breaking with tradition. And they didn't like change. And they most definitely didn't like a woman telling them what to do.

Everyone had told her that convincing these officials as with all other decision-makers she had to influence would take more than skill and strength of purpose. She was the outsider, just as her buildings were. On the edge, confronting other people's notions of compliance and predictability and subservience.

She'd stayed late at her office working through the night as she always did. She was quietly confident, but it was an audacious design. Why couldn't she do what her mother had always told her to do—why couldn't she settle for less?

The community library was the biggest project she and her small team of fledgling architects had ever handled—and the most important. Books changed lives. Books made people better citizens. Books liberated people from their constrained lives.

Liberation. Freedom. Escape. She owed it to people. Her architecture was designed for everyday men and women—not the elite.

She had worked on the concept tirelessly, sacrificing the rest of her life. Architecture was her big love. *Her only love.* Work kept her guilt, and her anger and her shame at bay, she told herself ignoring the emptiness and longing that slopped in her belly, calling her a liar.

·　·　·

CLAIMED BY THE SHEIKH, book two in the True Love series
series available now from all good bookstores.

ABOUT THE AUTHOR

MOLLIE MATHEWS writes fun, sophisticated, passion-filled contemporary romance. She is known for her "sensual, beautiful, empowered stories enveloped in true romance" (5-star review). Her books have resonated with a global audience. She has been featured in magazines, television, and radio.

A former child and family therapist Mollie passionately believes in the power of romance to transform people's lives. She loves Mother Theresa's words, *"We are all pens in the hands of a writing God sending love letters to the world."*

Her stories are unashamedly positive, optimistic, full of fun and passion.

She is graduate of Victoria University, in Wellington, New Zealand and has given keynote speeches at romance writers conventions and international seminars.

Mollie follows the sun, dividing her time between New Zealand and exotic locations—wherever she intends setting her next romance novel. She lives with her very own romantic hero, Lorenzo—tall, dark, terribly handsome and fluent in Spanish!

Follow her on BookBub https://www.bookbub.com/authors/mollie-mathews and on her blog https://molliemathews.wordpress.com

and sign up for Mollie's newsletter at www.Molliemathews.com and receive her FREE gift.

BY MOLLIE MATHEWS

GEMSTONE BILLIONAIRE BRIDES:

*THE ITALIAN BILLIONAIRE'S CHRISTMAS
   BRIDE*

*THE ITALIAN BILLIONAIRE'S
   SCANDALOUS MARRIAGE*

*GEMSTONE BILLIONAIRES 2 BOOK-
   BUNDLE BOX SET*

*GEMSTONE BILLIONAIRES 3 BOOK-
   BUNDLE BOX SET*

PASSION DOWN UNDER:

MARRIED BY CHRISTMAS
BRIDE OF GOLD

TRUE LOVE:

FLIGHT of PASSION
CLAIMED by THE SHEIKH

PASSION DOWN UNDER SASSY SHORT
STORIES:

TWIST OF FATE
LOVE ME FOREVER
LOVE ME AS I AM
FOREVER AND ALWAYS
THE LIGHTKEEPER'S LOVER
PASSION DOWN UNDER 2 BOOK-BUNDLE
      BOX SET (Books 1 & 2)

First Published 2019

First New Zealand eBook and Paperback Edition 2018

Cover Design: © German Creative

ISBN eBook 978-0-9941410-8-8

ISBN Print 978-0-9941410-6-4

Published by

Blue Orchid Publishing

New Zealand

Visit www.molliemathews.com to read more about all our books and to buy them. You will also find features, author interviews and news of author events, and you can sign up for e-newsletters so that you're always first to hear about our new releases.

❀ Created with Vellum

www.ingramcontent.com/pod-product-compliance
Lightning Source LLC
Chambersburg PA
CBHW021701110726
47902CB00007B/2022